There Time

J.J. GREEN

Copyright © 2015

Copyright for this story is held by J.J. Green. All rights reserved.

No part of this book may be reproduced in any written, electronic, recording, or photocopying without written permission of the publisher or author. The exception would be in the case of brief quotations embodied in the critical articles of reviews and pages where permission is specifically granted by the publisher or author.

This book is a work of fiction. Names, characters, places, and incidents are products of the author's imagination or are used fictitiously. Any resemblance to actual events, locales, or persons living or dead, is entirely coincidental.

First Edition.

ISBN: **1515227324**
ISBN-13: **978-1515227328**

Cover Design by James, GoOnWrite.com

This collection uses British spellings.

ALSO BY J.J. GREEN

DEATH SWITCH
A NOVELLA

DAWN FALCON
A FANTASY COLLECTION

***

J.J. GREEN'S WORK ALSO APPEARS IN

TAIWAN TALES

&

NIGHT MARKET

CONTENTS

There Comes a Time	1
Ice Dreamer	23
Tread Lightly	39
Robot Relations	56
What Poppa Pills Did For Me	67
Why I Chose You	72
The Last Days of Duane Dayton	77
Breathing Space	92
Red Ochre	121
Return of the Prodigals	136
Never in Fear Fly to the Woods	144

If you enjoy *There Comes a Time* and would like to hear about other J.J. Green books, new releases, advanced reader opportunities and other interesting stuff, sign up to the mailing list here:

https://infinitebook.wordpress.com/

You'll receive a free ebook fantasy collection, *Dawn Falcon*.

(We won't send spam or pass on your details to a third party.)

There Comes a Time

When Caris came through she fell to her knees on thick leaf mould. Her hands thudded into the ground before her, sinking into the damp, decaying surface. Humidity prickled her skin with sweat. She lifted her heavy head and tried to focus her swimming vision. Shades of green and brown danced and shimmered, then sharpened and slotted into perspective. She staggered up and checked behind her. Ferns, vines, trees, scattered pools and striations of light, the same as the scene in front. A din of cicada, frog and bird calls assaulted her ears. She rubbed her hands down her thighs and wiped the sweat from her face. One hour. First, she should try to find some clothes.

Caris was no expert on trees, but she guessed the largest ones she saw as she stepped through the jungle were more than forty to fifty years old. She was supposed to be in Stockbridge, Florida. Had they got the coordinates wrong? Or was it possible Stockbridge no longer existed? Without a trail to follow, she headed downhill. Downhill led to water, and water usually meant people.

She eased through the thick undergrowth. Damp foliage, branches and vines soon covered her bare skin in grime and a haphazard pattern of scratches, grazes. Hand-sized spiders hung suspended in webs between the trees, and snakes and lizards slithered and scattered at her approach. Rivulets of sweat cut tracks along her sooty skin.

The first building Caris saw appeared to rear up at her, it was so well hidden by the jungle. A half-crumbled wall, a vacant door and window frames collapsed and rotting. She stepped inside. The building was open to the sky. The remains of the roof littered the ground, and strong saplings sprouted among the cracked tiles and decayed timbers. She searched among the ruins. Anything and anyone that had once existed in the house was long gone. Nothing was there but dead leaves and the burgeoning life of the forest.

Caris wondered how much time had passed. Half an hour? Forty-five minutes? She fumed at her superiors. What was she supposed to discover in just sixty minutes? Leaving the building, she surveyed the trees around her. One had a branch just above head height, and was taller than the others as well. She jumped and pulled herself up onto the branch. Grabbing vines, branches and knots she hauled herself up the tree until, balancing on a thin, springy branch and gripping fistfuls of shoots, she pushed through the canopy.

Sunlight pierced her eyes. Adjusting to the increased light, she became aware of a cloud of butterflies spanning the treetops as far as she could see. Floating, hovering, gliding; deep browns, purples and blacks shimmered, iridescent in the sunlight. Butterflies alighted on her, as if she were just another part of the canopy, and she grinned in delight. But puzzlement took over. Shading her eyes and looking into the far distance, all she could see was an ocean of leaves and butterflies like foam on the waves.

A sudden thought struck her. Was her hour nearly up? And if it was, she was about 75 feet above the ground. Would she be dragged back at the same height? She slid off the branch and descended rapidly, skittering monkey-like down the branches. Cursing as she acquired more scratches and bruises, she prepared mentally for a fall from mid-air. Fifty-foot drop. She might live if she fell from here. Twenty-five feet. She could get away with broken legs. Fifteen feet. If she executed a perfect parachute roll, she might walk away.

They grabbed her as she jumped from the bottom branch. Caris' stomach lurched and her knees slammed into hard tile. Vomit forced its way up her throat. She spewed it out and pitched forward. Her head struck the floor and she slid through the pool of vomit in a dead faint.

***

"Should we contact someone? Husband? Relatives?" asked Lieutenant Merritt.

General Nancarrow shook his head. "She's single. No boyfriend. No close relatives. That's one of the reasons she was chosen. Less chance of her letting something slip." The two army officers were standing at Caris' bedside in a windowless hospital room.

"Okay, I'll ask the nurses to keep an eye on her so there's someone around when she wakes up."

"Thanks for taking over as her psych support at such short notice. We need to be careful. She'll most likely be groggy and disoriented. We can't risk her saying anything that sounds odd. You know what I mean. And we need her ready for debriefing as soon as possible. So stick around, is what I'm saying."

Merritt nodded and the general left. The lieutenant looked down at the unconscious figure on the bed. She had short hair and her thin face was bruised and scratched. She didn't look at all like his mental image of a time traveler—tough, exotic and strange. She looked very ordinary and vulnerable.

A screen was embedded on the wall next to the bed, and Merritt scrolled through the information. Twenty-six years old. Parents dead, one from a drug overdose and the other in a bank hold up, as the perpetrator. Foster care kid in numerous homes. Enlisted at sixteen. Exemplary record of active service. Prodigious technical talent. Merritt scrolled ahead to the psych evaluation. He scanned it, and went back to the personal history. Strange. Her psych score was nearly perfect, which was completely at odds with her upbringing.

He glanced down at Caris and started. Her eyes were open and watching him.

"See anything interesting?"

"Hi, Caris. Glad to see you're awake. I'm Lieutenant Merritt." He took out his ID and showed it to her. "I'm here to make sure you're okay. How are you feeling?"

"Like death."

Merritt drew up a chair and sat down. "It'll ease over the next few days, I expect. Time travel must be like an exaggerated version of long haul flights. You're experiencing a form of jet lag. Or time lag, I suppose I should say."

"Hmph. So ... you aren't a medic. You're the new psychiatrist?"

"Psych support officer. Hungry?"

"Nope. What happened to Lieutenant Norris?"

"He's in intensive care. Stroke. Thirsty? How about a drink?"

"That's for me, right?" Caris looked at the jug of water and tumbler on the table next to her bed. "I'll be okay." There was a silence. "Look, you don't have to hang around. I'm okay. I won't say anything to anyone, if that's what's worrying you."

Merritt stood up to leave, but hesitated.

"Really, I'm okay," said Caris. "I'm sure you have plenty to do."

Merritt leaned toward her and said in a low voice, "Caris, you've just been a hundred years into the future. Don't you want to talk about how you're feeling? You know, share? It must have been quite an experience."

Caris thought a moment then said, "No, I'm good."

Merritt tilted his head and smiled. The woman seemed perfectly calm and relaxed. He regarded her battered face. Gel coated the worst cuts, holding the edges together and healing them. In a few days' time, under the hospital's state-of-the-art care, she would be as good as new. And the physical effects of the first extended journey in time would have left as few effects on her body as it appeared to have left on her mind.

"You sure you don't need anything?"

Caris shook her head, smiled and gave Merritt a thumbs-up.

The next time he saw her was at the debriefing. She stood in uniform before an assembly of most of the highest-ranking military personnel in the country. Merritt scrutinized her facial expression and body language. She appeared entirely unfazed.

Nancarrow stood and turned to the other officers. "I propose we let Corporal Elliott tell us her account, then ask questions. Are we in agreement?"

Caris spoke for twenty minutes, giving each detail of her experience from start to finish, describing the physical geography, flora and fauna she encountered, the single, tumble-down building she had found, and the view of endless jungle she had seen. A tutting admiral interrupted.

"There's surely been some kind of error here. That sounds nothing at all like Stockbridge. Is there something wrong in the calculations, or a problem with the machine? We must have sent her somewhere different. We sent her to the Amazon, or some such other place."

Nancarrow stood again. "Can we wait for Corporal Elliot to finish?"

"General Nancarrow, I'm done. It was at that moment I was retrieved," said Caris.

"Right. Thank you, Corporal. Well, let's commence questions, then."

Merritt watched Caris. The officers fired off questions, interrupting one another and repeating themselves. The volume of noise in the room rose and petty squabbles broke out as each tried to make him- or herself heard. A heated argument on the possibility of global warming creating a jungle in the area broke out. Caris answered each question patiently, giving the same information over and over again. Merritt would have expected anyone else to experience frustration, but Caris only looked bored.

He took her back to the hospital for a final physical exam before she was discharged. The autocab whipped through the streets, equidistant from every other vehicle.

"Caris, I have a question for you about your experience, if you don't mind."

"Shoot."

"How did you feel about it?"

Caris sighed. "Look, I know you're just doing your job, but I'm okay. I'm not going to have a mental breakdown or anything. I'm not like that."

"I know. I'm your psych support, remember? I didn't mean that. I meant, what was it like, being there? A hundred years in the future. I mean, wow."

"Hmph." Caris watched the streets of Stockbridge fleeting past. Clean, neat, sharp-edged and modern. Glass-fronted stores glinted in the sunlight. The pavements were even, the signs bright. She thought back to the expanse of jungle that, as far as she could tell, would take its place in one hundred year's time. She turned to Merritt. "You know what? I felt great. It was beautiful."

"Yeah?"

"Yeah. It was alive, you know? So alive. I've never seen anything like it. It was how it must have been before we took over the planet. It's kind of nice to know there comes a time when we return the Earth to a natural state."

Merritt tried to imagine.

"Hey, you're okay, you know," said Caris.

"Huh?"

"The rest of them, they didn't care. All they wanted

to know was where all the people had gone. No one else tried to understand what it was like. How it felt to be there."

***

The second time they sent her she had two hours. A pig, a dog and a monkey had survived four hours in the future, so there was no reason to suppose a human wouldn't survive half that, they had reasoned and she had agreed. Caris sat down to be transported. The last thing she saw was Lieutenant Merritt's face through the observation screen. He looked anxious, poor guy. Anyone would think it was him travelling into the future. Then came the dizziness and blurred vision.

The Stockbridge of fifty years hence surrounded Caris. It was a wrecked town. The buildings that were still standing were advanced in the process of disintegration. Weeds and saplings opened wide cracks in the sidewalk and roads. Concluding it wouldn't be safe to enter any buildings, as they all seemed in a state of imminent collapse, she leaned in through the windows. Rats scuttled away at her approach.

Apart from the rats, the place seemed devoid of life. It was silent and nothing moved in the streets. Caris walked to the places she knew, the sun hot on her skin. The sports stadium was a shell and the shopping center had clearly at some point collapsed in spectacular fashion. Now it was little more than a heap of concrete blocks, glass, rusting girders and dust. She remembered a small post office a few blocks downtown and headed there.

What remained of the post office was in no firmer state than the other buildings, but Caris had to risk entering it if she wanted to try and find out what had happened. Piles of yellowed, decaying papers covered the floor. Letters, postcards, bills, advertising. She dug down to reach less weathered paper on the lower layers, but they were sodden mush. The print on the papers on top was so worn and rain-damaged it was illegible. Caris lifted telephone receivers and listened to the silence. The computer screens were dead and cracked, the wiring rotten.

Caris estimated she had about forty-five minutes left. Enough time to get to the government buildings if she ran. Her orders were to bring back information on future technologies and survey the broader aspects of civilian life. If there was anyone left at all, they could be there. She ran through the empty streets, the sound of her footsteps echoing from the vacant, desolate buildings. A faint tingle of unease ran down her spine. The absence of life intruded into her senses, and the hairs rose on her neck. The empty windows seemed full of eyes, watching her. What had happened to all the people? Where had they gone? The derelict buildings seemed to be burgeoning with their ghosts, willing her to find out.

Caris stopped, resting her hands on her knees. She closed her eyes and shook her head. She stood straight and looked around at the buildings, willing the illusion away. Closing their eyes, the ghosts retreated.

In another five minutes she was at the central offices. The wide glass doors had shattered and glass crumbs adorned the grassy weeds growing through the sidewalk. Placing her bare feet carefully, Caris stepped inside. The ground floor had retained its ceiling, and the interior was dark. Caris waited a moment to allow her eyes to adjust, but she knew she had only a few minutes left. Squinting into the shadows, she walked through the reception area. Her foot caught, and she stumbled. Turning back to see what had tripped her, she gasped. Rotten clothes hung from a skeleton. She stood, and swiveled, surveying the room. Similar heaps were scattered across it. Bones and skulls, yellowed and stained, made disorganized piles on the floor. Caris' hackles rose as she felt herself grabbed back.

After the vomiting came oblivion.

***

Merritt offered to take Caris out to eat after the debriefing, and he wasn't surprised when she accepted. Her demeanor was altered, and it wasn't due to the arguing, shouting and chaos of the meeting. She was preoccupied and anxious, and he noticed her hands trembled. She was as laconic at dinner as she had ever been, however, and they ate in silence for a while.

"You want to talk about it?" he asked. When she didn't hear his question for the second time, he placed his hand on hers.

"Hey," she said, pulling her hand away.

Merritt raised his hands. "Just trying to get your attention."

"Oh. Sorry."

"It sometimes helps to talk things through."

Caris sighed and closed her eyes. "I know. I do know that. It's just I'm not used to ..."

" ... feeling bad about stuff?" Merritt offered.

"Feeling bad about stuff. That's a good way of putting it."

"It's normal. Hell, if I'd been thrown into the future and dragged back again I'd be a wreck."

"Lieutenant Merritt— "

"Call me Ben."

"Ben," she said. "Ben, I've seen death. I've seen it happen to enemies and to friends. And I've stared it right in the face. Death's terrible, you know, but it is what it is. It comes to all of us. But there ... that place .... Ben, there was nothing. Nothing but rats, and silence." She shuddered. "And it's the future. That's what's coming, right?"

"No one knows, Caris. It's a possible future, certainly. But we don't know whether it's the only one. Some theories say time is already complete and part of the physical universe—that we're only experiencing the illusion of travelling through it. Others say there are multitudes of futures, each decided whenever there's a choice of possibilities. That's one of the things they're trying to find out, by sending people like you through. Only ..."

"What?"

"The individuals that go through must be psychologically robust. You know the transporter only works for living things, so you can't take any recording equipment with you, and you can't bring any artifacts back. The reports you give must be reliable, and not influenced by your mental state -"

"Are you telling me I'm not fit to take the next run?"

"Caris, no one even knows whether there will be another run."

"I'm fine, Ben. I'm fine. Come on, don't tell them I'm

not fit. You should have seen that place. We've got to find out what happened. So we can stop it happening. Don't tell them I'm not fit, please."

"Caris, as far as I'm concerned you're experiencing a normal reaction to what you saw. You just need to talk it through. I don't think you're unstable at all. But ... talk, okay?"

While the President, the Cabinet, the generals and admirals debated and argued over how to proceed with investigating the future, Caris and Ben met daily for counselling sessions. Caris talked about what she had seen and how she had felt in the future Stockbridge, about her time in the army, the tours she'd been on, and her childhood going from foster home to foster home.

"Do you want to talk about how it felt? A new home, a new family every year or even more often?" asked Ben one day.

Caris shrugged. "It wasn't so bad. They were okay—the foster parents, I mean. Others had it worse than me."

Ben laughed and put down his pen.

"Did I say something funny?" asked Caris.

"Caris, I'm sorry. I'm not laughing at you, but I just

don't understand how you've coped so well with everything that's happened to you. I've counseled soldiers with severe psychological disorders, PTSD—the works. And they haven't experienced half the trauma you have. I don't get it."

Caris looked out the counselling office window. "I don't know, Ben. Maybe it's different for some people. Maybe my experiences brought out the best in me. Maybe if I'd had an easy life I'd be a wreck."

"It's an interesting idea. And it's interesting talking to you, Caris."

She smiled and he smiled back. Their eyes locked a fraction too long, then they both looked away.

"You know, Ben, I never really understood the point of counselling before," Caris said. "but I needed these sessions, after my last assignment. They've helped."

Ben looked down at his notes.

"Is something wrong?" asked Caris.

"Caris, please believe me when I say it's nothing to do with anything you've said or done, but I have to step down as your counsellor. I'll find a replacement for you. A good one."

"What? Why? If it isn't me, why are you stepping down? What's wrong?"

"I'm afraid my professional code forbids me telling you that."

"Then don't tell me as my counsellor. Tell me as a friend."

"Caris, I can't be your friend, either."

Caris looked at Ben across the low coffee table that separated them. Moments passed, and he refused to meet her gaze. She got up, walked halfway to the door, then stopped. She walked back and stood next to Ben's chair. As he looked up at her, opening his mouth to speak, she stooped and kissed him.

***

A low moaning was the first thing Caris heard when she went through the third time. Ben's smiling face through the transporter room glass was still in her mind as, blinking her vision clear, she saw movement ahead. A beggar, staggering toward her. She sidestepped, but he grabbed her arm and pushed his face into hers.

"Help, help me," he breathed.

Caris turned her head to escape his foul exhalation and grabbed his arms to hold him away from her. She looked around, but the street was empty except for the two of them. She pushed the beggar gently away and stepped back.

"I'm sorry, but, as you can see, I need to find some clothes." She walked quickly away. When she had turned a corner, she slipped down the side path next to a house with no cars on the drive. Trying the back door, she was surprised to find it open. The house was empty, and it looked as though the family had left in a hurry. Dishes thick with mould filled the sink, and an unemptied rubbish bin sent out a stench. Upstairs, she put on clothes she found among the many left in the open wardrobes.

She looked out the bedroom window. It was about three in the afternoon but the street was empty. No one in the yards, no cars, no pedestrians, not even any kids playing on the sidewalk. Caris felt her knees buckle and she sat down on the unmade bed. The beggar, the hastily vacated house, the deserted street. This was only two years in the future. Whatever disaster was going to befall them, it was going to happen within two years. They had *two years* left?

For a while, Caris sat on the bed, unable to move. She looked out at the blue sky, sunshine and clouds, the silence pounding her ears. Then she stirred. Perhaps, if she could find out what had happened, they could put it right. They might be able to prevent the disaster happening. Ben had said there might be many possible futures. She needed to make at least one future safe.

She ran down the stairs and found the home

computer, but it was dead. She flipped a light switch and cursed. The electricity was off. She could not access the autocab system even if it was still running. She would have to travel on foot again.

Caris jogged from house to house, knocking at doors and peering in windows. At one place two dogs barked and yelped. The sun sank lower. Caris ran through the street after street. She could not find a single human being. Then she saw the front door to a house standing open. As she drew nearer, she smelled a terrible stench. She knew what it meant, but went inside to investigate anyway.

Downstairs was empty, so she went up to the bedrooms. A busy hum of flies came from the master bedroom. A brief look inside revealed what might once have been an old couple, lying in each others' arms. She ran to the next house. The front door was unlocked. Opening it, she was greeted with the same stench, and at the next house, and the next.

Caris ran down the street. She stopped and sank to her knees. For a moment she hugged herself, rocking, then forced herself to her feet. Blinking back tears, she looked around, got her bearings, then set off at a sprint. As she neared the hospital, she noticed banners draped across the signs. Hospital full, they said, in large, capital letters. Please return home. Wait for assistance.

Panting, Caris slowed to a walk. The hospital grounds

were deserted. The ambulance bay was open. The automatic doors to the reception area stood apart. Caris stepped through and a nurse in a surgical mask and dirty scrubs ran up.

"Who are you? Have you come from the government? Have you brought supplies? Are they going to turn the electricity back on?"

"I—No, I'm sorry."

"You're a patient? We can't take any more. We can't help you. You have to go home."

"I'm not a patient. I just want to know what's going on."

"You want to—? Where have you been?" The nurse's eyes grew wide above her mask. "If you haven't been in contact with anyone, you might stand a chance. Get away. Get away now. Go back wherever you came from."

"Please. Tell me what's happening first."

"It's a virus. It takes a few months to kill you, but it's deadly, and extremely contagious. Skin contact, breath, anything. No one knows where it came from, but it started here in Stockbridge and it's spreading everywhere. If you haven't touched anyone with it, you might be okay."

"If I haven't ..." Caris remembered the beggar. "No. No ...." She looked at the sun. How long did she have? Five minutes? Ten? She pushed past the nurse.

"Don't touch me! Where are you going?"

Caris started stripping her clothes. "I need a pen. And a scalpel."

***

Ben waited for Caris to reappear. Two hours in the future didn't mean anything in the present. For him, it had only been five minutes since she left. One second the transporter was empty; the next, she was there. He stared. She was lying on the floor, writing covering her from head to toe. Blood seeped from her wrists. The guards at the door tried to stop him but he was too fast. He shoved them aside and ran into the room. He grabbed Caris' limp form and pulled her into his arms. Her face and lips were white, lifeless.

"Caris ..."

He heard a voice vaguely. "Step back, Lieutenant."

Hands pulled at him, dragging him away. Caris' body slipped from his grasp and slid onto the floor, her head lolling.

He tried to speak but nothing would come out. Avoiding Caris' glazed, vacant eyes, he read the writing on her body. It made no sense. The same three words written over and over again. *Don't touch me. Don't touch me. Don't touch me.*

Ice Dreamer

Prussis gingerly lifted the large, metal, cylindrical container out of the refrigeration unit. It was heavy, and the fluid inside made it difficult to keep evenly balanced. She slid it onto the dusty bench and plugged the sensor wires into their inlets. She turned to the monitor. Good. The temperature inside was at exactly six degrees Celsius. Warm-up was progressing nicely.

The circulation machine sat nearby. Prussis pulled two small soft plastic tubes from it and attached them to the valves on either side of the container. Turning the machine on, she programmed it to a one degree increase per hour for the next 26 hours. She sat back. In the old, disused lab, the sunlight was shining low through the windows, lighting up motes in the air. The circulation machine whirred softly.

There was a click as the lab door opened and Herna, Prussis' supervisor, came in. Prussis felt a wave of embarrassment and annoyance. The inevitable comment came.

"You're not warming up another of those dead heads are you?"

Prussis decided to maintain her dignity in silence. Hertna snorted.

"How many does that make it now? A hundred? More? You'd think you'd have learned your lesson. It's just going to be another pile of mush, you know. What on earth makes you think this one'll be any different?"

"Not that it's any business of yours, but *this* one happens to have been preserved before legal death."

"Really? So?"

Prussis turned pointedly away and pretended to adjust the controls on the machines.

"Actually, I didn't know they'd done any like that ... Can I have a look?"

"No, it's important not to violate the integrity of the preservation chamber ... it's ... stop it ... get off!"

Hertna had marched over and was trying to unscrew the lid. There was a short scuffle, but Hertna was the stronger opponent and Prussis was too concerned about disturbing the container contents to fight strongly. They both gazed down at the grey, shaven scalp beneath the clear nutrient solution. A mild disturbance stirred the surface as slowly warming, oxygenated liquid gently circled the chamber. *You have to credit the cryogenic engineers of the twenty-first century*, thought Prussis. *The head didn't look more than a day or two old. A bit wrinkly, like it'd been in a swimming pool for several hours too long, but not too bad.*

"Humph!" said Hertna. "Looks the same as the others. Dead meat. Make sure you chuck it before it starts to stink the place out." She picked up her file and strode out.

***

The next day, Prussis managed to sneak away from her lab work to check the head, now reaching the end of its warming cycle. The temperature gauge read 32 degrees. So far, so good. But then, all the others had been repaired and warmed up as they were supposed to be too, only to end up as hamburger ingredient.

Sighing, Prussis set the machine to a half degree increase per hour, to stop at 36 degrees. She also started up the brain communication unit. Might as well go through with it.

Later, after work, she went upstairs to the warmed up head awaiting her. She took sandwiches, expecting a long evening ahead. Settling down next to the container, she powered up her interface to pass the time. *Science: 99% boring tasks, 1% ... well, disappointment mostly,* she thought.

Three hours later, the circulation machine pinged. At 36 degrees, if the head was going to return to life it was now or ... soon, maybe. Prussis put her interface down and spoke into the communicator. Her message would manifest as an extremely mild electrical impulse through the tissues of the brain, stimulating auditory perception.

"Hello? Hello? Can you hear me?" She glanced at the monitor. Nothing.

"Hello? Testing, one, two, three. Hello?" Still nothing. Of course. But Prussis was determined not to give up immediately. The brain had not worked in a long time. It might take a while to come back online. She picked up her interface and began browsing websites, looking for a new pet miniature elephant. She had wanted one for a while and now seemed a good time to buy, what with the prices coming down and everything.

"Bloody hell!" A voice exploded in the room. Prussis fell off her stool then hastily scrambled to her feet, looking round wildly for the source. But there was no one else there. There was only one possibility. She leaned towards the microphone of the communicator.

"Er ... hello?"

"What the hell's going on? Where am I? Why's it all dark, and why can't I move? Have you lot got me pinned down or something? Let me up immediately and turn the bloody lights on, or I'll sue this place for every penny it's worth."

"Oh, oh, oh my god. Oh my god. Hello? Are you, are you ... " Prussis hastily sorted through her document files to the sparse data download she had for the preserved patient. But, as with most of them, all she had was a registration number, and the circumstances of preservation.

"Are you ... ummm ...."

"Never mind that, put the lights on. And someone had better bloody well tell me what's going on."

"Oh, oh ... well ... it's a bit difficult to explain ...."

"Listen, darling, you better do your bloody best. I haven't got time to be lying around. I want answers. Now."

"Oh, oh, okay." Prussis thought madly. All the times she had contemplated this event, this was not quite the conversation she had imagined. "Um, well, um ... what's the last thing you remember?"

"I thought it was me asking the questions here? I

want to know ...I demand to know ... oh, wait ...." The communicator fell silent. "Hold on. Oh ... oh, yes ... oh, right, I see. Right." There was another silence that went on for some time. Partly to be sure she was not dreaming, Prussis spoke into the microphone again.

"Hello? Are you okay?"

"Yes, yes, I'm all right. It's just, quite a lot to take in, you know. Just need a minute, to gather my thoughts, that kind of thing."

"Okay, I understand." Prussis sat back. What should she do? In all the many attempts she had made to bring a brain back to life, she had never bothered to find out what you were supposed to do if you actually succeeded. Was there even a procedure in place? Maybe there had been fifty years ago when it was first attempted, but since no one had ever managed it, any supporting guidelines were not easy to come by.

"Oy, you!" came the voice again. "I've got a few questions."

"My name's Prussis."

"I don't care what your bloody name is. Now, tell me, what year is this?"

Prussis didn't answer.

"Did you hear me? What year are we in?"

She remained silent.

"Oh, all right, Priscilla, or whatever ..."

"Prussis."

"Prussis, Prussis, Got it. So, what year is it, Prussis, my dear?"

"It's 2278."

"Bloody hell! 2278? 2278? I don't believe it. That's ... that's nearly 250 years in the future!"

"Well, no, not exactly, is it? I mean this is the present, and you're ... by the way, who are you? What's your name?"

"What's my name? You mean you don't know? Who are you? Where am I?"

"Well ... " This was going to be tricky. "Well, you're at a pharmaceutical company on the site of the cryogenics lab that preserved you. I'm afraid I don't have much information about you. The data's corrupted ... and ... well ... no one bothers trying to bring back preserved people anymore. They gave up years ago. That you've woken up ... it's marvellous. Everyone thought it was impossible. I do it as a hobby, trying to resurrect—I mean revive—the cryogenically preserved. I never succeeded until now." She did not add that the head had nearly ended up in the incinerator, nor that the only reason it had not was because the CEO was a friend of the family and she had persuaded him to let her conduct some personal experiments.

"A what! A hobby? I paid four million for this. Four million! State-of-the-art preservation they told me. Latest technology. Guaranteed revival. *Guaranteed!*" Prussis thought that if it were possible for the communicator to explode, it would.

"Well, to be fair, you have been revived," said Prussis. This was, after all, just a head in a box.

"Don't you get smart with me! What about all the other poor idiots who fell for it? You said they gave up trying to revive people. That means no one else survived. It means I must be the only one. The only one ...."

"The only one ... so far," said Prussis.

The brain didn't reply at first. Then,

"The name's Dave. Dave Hepplethwaite."

"Oh, right. Pleased to meet you, Dave."

"I had a wife. Nora. Nora Hepplethwaite. I don't suppose you know what happened to her?"

"No, but ... I can try and find out." But Prussis knew there was not a hope in hell of locating the woman's brain, assuming it still existed.

"Good ... I mean ... I'd appreciate it."

"No problem."

Prussis waited a while. She checked the time. Twenty past eleven. She thought she should really tell someone what had happened. Probably the CEO. Face to face. She suddenly realised that even *she* had not ever actually believed she could bring a twenty-first century person back to life.

"Dave?"

"Yeah?"

"Dave, I was thinking, maybe I should leave you alone for a while, to, you know, think things over."

"You're going?"

"Well, I understand this must be a massive shock to you, and ...."

"I'd rather you didn't. I mean, it's all dark here ...."

"Oh, yes, of course. Well, I'll stick around for a while, shall I?"

"Yeah. I've got a few questions too."

***

They began to talk. Dave wanted to know what the world was like, who was in power, how people lived. Prussis told him about what was generally considered the greatest achievement of the twenty-third century: the SEEERS, a group of top scientists, engineers, economists and ethicists who guided world affairs; she told him about the abolition of countries and the free availability of energy, education and health care to every human being. She explained how people lived in small communities in natural surroundings; how crime was unusual and how there was no longer any real distinction between rich and poor.

Dave's curiosity was huge and she was unable to answer many of his questions. She had no idea what had happened to many of the landmarks of his time, or the international corporations, or the rich and famous people. The notable figures that she knew of from his time, that history had recorded, were unknown to him.

They talked on. Prussis sat, leaning forward on the bench, her chin in her hand, her face close to the communication unit. The sensation of unreality was almost palpable to her, talking to another human being who had last been conscious more than 250 years ago. She had many questions of her own but Dave never gave her any opportunity to ask them.

The sky outside the window lightened, and still

Dave's questions came. What did people eat now? The fact that humankind had become vegetarian seemed to annoy him. And transportation? How did people get around? Small cars for short distances and public transport to go further? He sounded disappointed. And what did they do to relax? He did not seem to think that informal dinners with friends and evening classes sounded much fun.

The world outside was waking up. Prussis rubbed her eyes. She knew she really should go and inform the CEO about all of this.

"Dave, look, I'm sorry, but it's morning. We've been talking for hours. I have to go and tell someone about you so I can find out what to do next."

"That's another question I have ..."

Prussis sighed.

"What happens now, then? What's next for me, eh?"

"Well, like I said, you're the first person who's ever been successfully revived, so it's not clear, but I would have thought we will grow you a new body and either transplant your brain or read its information to program a fresh one. There'll be some loss of data from what I've heard. But it's probably better to go with the new brain anyway, I'd say."

"A new body, eh? ...."

"Yes, a new body. You'll be able to walk around, eat, talk, sleep, for the first time in 250 years. Won't that be wonderful? It's a good world nowadays, Dave. You'll love it. And, when you've fully recovered, I imagine the world's historians will be clamouring to talk to you."

Beams of early sunlight were filtering into the room. *A new day in the life of Dave Hepplethwaite,* thought Prussis.

But Dave was silent.

"Dave?"

" ... I—Nah, I think ... I think I'll give it a miss."

"I ... I'm sorry?"

"I said thanks but no thanks. I'll pass on it, if you don't mind."

"What? The new brain?"

"Nah, the whole deal."

Prussis stood up and leaned toward the communicator, her hands gripping the bench.

"What? You mean, you mean, after all this, you don't want to live again? Why? I mean, what's the point? Why did you go to all the trouble of being preserved, and paying millions of whatever money there was in those days, to just give up now?"

"To be frank, Priscilla, or whatever your name is, your world doesn't sound very interesting for a bloke like me."

"Not interesting?" Prussis' voice rose to a squeak. "But ... but ... civilisation is much more advanced than it was in your time! We've cured cancer, ended wars ... what do you mean *not interesting*? Do you think starving to death is interesting? Or people murdering each other? Or ... or ... or dying of a heart attack?"

"Yeah, look, it's not your fault you don't get it, but where I come from, I'm an important man. Was, I mean. Wealthy. Nice lifestyle. Of course, it all had to come to an end. It's only natural. But, I thought, why not try to live a bit longer? Life's too much fun for it all to stop now."

"I thought, me and Nora, we could have a whale of a time fifty years on. Lots of lovely money through appreciation of my assets, a cure for Nora's MS. We could have the time of our lives. Fine dining, luxury accommodation, holidays, the lot. Eating slop and poodling about in poncy little cars isn't exactly what I had in mind. No offence. What's more, from the sound of it, I'd never fit in. I'd be an anap ... an anat ... an ...."

"An anachronism?"

"That's the word."

"So ... so what are you going to do?"

"It's not what *I'm* going to do, it's what *you're* going to do, dearie. I'm assuming you rigged me up to something to get me going again? Well, just turn me off, then. Easy."

"You want me to disconnect you, so your brain ... you ... you'll die?"

"Yep, that's the idea. You've got it in one."

"But, you're the very first head I've managed to revive! You're the only head that's ever been revived!"

"Now you're not going to get all selfish on me, are you? It is my head after all. I think I should be able to do what I want with it, don't you? ... Unless ... "

Prussis waited ... was he going to change his mind?

"You aren't going to be able to find Nora for me, are you ... Not the remotest chance, is there, eh?"

"Well, no."

"Thought not. So. Let's not get sentimental about it. Just pull the plug or whatever it is you have to do. No point in dragging it out."

"But ... but ... Dave .... I—I was just getting to know you." Prussis' shoulders slumped and she sniffed.

"Oh dear, oh dear. Look, it's all right ... I'm just going to go back to how I was before. Which is fine. I rolled the dice and I lost, that's all. Nothing to worry about. Best be brave and get it over with."

***

Half an hour later, Hertna marched in.

"You're here early," she said. "I thought I was the only one. Checking up on that head again? How's it doing? Warmed up yet?"

"Yes, it's warmed up."

"No sign of anything, I suppose?"

Prussis opened her mouth and closed it again. Then she said, "No, no sign."

"Are you all right? Your eyes look red. Not enough sleep. You think about these heads too much, Prussis. You might as well give up. You're never going to get one working again."

Hertna deposited her tray of agar plates.

"You are going to send it to the incinerator now, aren't you? I can't stand it if they start to smell."

She pushed the door open and left, muttering, "What a waste of time."

Tread Lightly

Geoffrey Finch's first buyer was a young woman, a mother perhaps, though thankfully she had not brought her child with her. Even Geoff could not have stomached that. They met at the local park on a sunny Sunday afternoon when the crowds would provide anonymity. Long grass and weedy saplings also helped obscure them from view.

At the pre-arranged spot beneath an ancient, diseased elm, Geoff sat down and pretended to admire the view, though it consisted of little more than scrubby undergrowth, weeds and overgrown trees. The legislation prohibiting unnecessary cutting or destruction of plant life had been enacted several years previously. He scratched his roughly cut, grey beard. A few moments later the woman arrived and sat separately, but close enough for a whispered conversation to take place as they looked in opposite directions.

"You're Steff?" the woman asked. Geoff had thought it safer to use a false name.

"Yes. You got the money?"

"Seven hundred. In here." The woman moved the newspaper she was holding from one hand to the other.

Geoff said at a normal volume, "Excuse me, could I borrow your newspaper?"

The woman turned and smiled.

"Sure," she said, handing it over.

Geoff opened the thin, smudged sheets. A small pile of bills lay in the centre. He decided counting the money would be too easy for onlookers to see. It looked about right. The woman would not cheat him if she wanted more. Geoff lowered his voice again.

"I'll put the package down and leave."

"How do I know you're not tricking me?"

"What do you want me to do? Get some out here in broad daylight?"

"Okay, okay."

Geoff was not a criminal by nature. He saw the need for laws, and all his life he had obeyed them. A veteran of the Food Wars, his moral code had been honed in the Texan desert fighting Right to Eaters. That had been a long time ago, and in a country far away, but his philosophy had not changed: if a thing did not harm people or living, feeling creatures, it was all right by him. But as he had grown older, the new laws made less and less sense to him, and he could not understand how the popular thinking of his youth had resulted in this strange, unfamiliar world he found himself living in.

And so Geoff Finch found himself committing one of the most serious crimes in the book.

Sweat trickled down his forehead, and he started to reconsider the whole idea. This could be a set-up. Maybe the woman wanted him to open the package and show her the contents to prove his guilt beyond doubt. Maybe she did not want him to walk away because he would have a better chance of escape. Once the package was out of his hands he could deny it was his at all. Unless they had him on tape. Geoff scanned the crowd and the surrounding landscape. He could not see anyone watching, nor anything that looked like a camera in the trees. But the place was busy, and it was hard to tell.

"Hey," said the woman, "you gonna leave that package or not? You scamming me?"

Geoff's heart was pounding. Hands trembling, he placed the package on the ground. He got unsteadily to his feet and set off, half walking, half running. He cursed his inability to saunter away as he had intended, but his feet seemed to have a mind of their own, carrying him swiftly, awkwardly, away.

He did not stop until he reached home. It was only when he was inside his house and his front door was closed and locked behind him that he allowed himself to relax. Leaning back against the closed door, he panted. He felt faint from the adrenaline coursing through his body.

A thought struck him. What if the police knew all about his little scheme and were waiting for him? His throat constricted, he held his breath and listened. Far off, stray dogs were barking at each other, and outside in the street a bicycle squeaked slowly past. Geoff realised that if the police were already on to him and were inside his house, they would have found everything and arrested him by now. He exhaled with relief.

He went into his bare, cold kitchen and slumped down on the single chair, putting the newspaper containing the money on the table. Despite the apparent success of his sale, Geoff was not pleased. He had started his cultivation scheme for personal use only, but electricity was so expensive he had realised he would not be able to sustain production without selling the surplus. Things would be so much safer if he could keep everything entirely to himself. At his age, he wasn't sure how long he could stand the stress of transactions similar to the one he had just experienced.

To take his mind off his fears, Geoff went to his attic to inspect his plants. The warm, green smell wafted out as he opened the door, relaxing and uplifting his spirits. It was a joy to see the living green growth he had created filling the cramped room. Geoff checked the lights. They shone as bright as day in rows across the tin-foil lined ceiling. None were burnt out, which was a relief. Light bulbs were costly and difficult to source.

Wandering among the tall stems and thick foliage, he checked the plants over. All seemed to be growing strongly. No pests or diseases had taken hold, which would have been unlikely in the entirely enclosed growing conditions, but Geoff enjoyed checking anyway. Like a father tending to his children, he caressed the long stems and leaves.

Calmed by half an hour spent inspecting his plants, Geoff decided to go down the local cafe and see if any of his friends had turned up. Carefully locking the attic door, he descended the stairs and put on the threadbare coat that he had left hanging over the banister. On his way to his front door he stopped, remembering the money on the kitchen table. The newspaper lay where he had left it. As he opened it out and tipped out the bills, a bold headline on the front page caught his eye: Microbe Rights Act Passed. Geoff turned the paper to read the article, squinting to read the faint grey print. Shaking his head, he folded the paper and put it in his coat pocket. He counted the money and found it was all there. Geoff took down a photo of his wife from the mantelpiece, hid the flimsy bills in the back of the frame, then put the photo back in place. He smiled back at the smiling image, kissed two fingers and put them on the image's lips, and left.

He walked his usual route to the cafe, side-stepping the areas that sapling trees and tall stands of weeds had invaded, watching carefully for dog mess, and going around large, deep puddles that never dried out and had developed into small, green ponds.

Opening the cafe door, Geoff saw the usual mix of familiar faces. He was pleased to see his old friend Charlie was there, sitting in the corner, looking a little older, a little more careworn, Geoff thought. He recalled the Charlie who had fought beside him, black-haired, young and strong. Comforting though it was to have friends who also remembered the old times, it was depressing to watch them age, knowing you were keeping pace with them.

Sitting at an ancient Formica table, Charlie was stirring his Syn tea. The only drink for sale.

"Charlie," said Geoff as he sat down.

Charlie looked up briefly. "Geoff." He looked down again at the pale brown liquid swirling around in the chipped cup.

"How's things?"

"Not bad."

They sat in silence, Geoff looking out the window and Charlie down into his cup, though neither really seemed to see what they were looking at. The waiter placed a cup of tea in front of Geoff and he took a sip. He grimaced.

"Tastes worse each time, I'm sure," he said.

Charlie laughed.

"Don't know what you mean by that," he said. "Can Syn tea taste worse?"

"Touche, my friend."

Both men sighed.

"Seen the latest?" Geoff asked.

"What's that?"

"You won't believe it."

"Try me."

"I tell you, they've really gone beyond the pale this time."

"You gonna tell me what it is or not?"

Geoff looked at Charlie from the corner of his eye. "Microbes," he said, then laughed and shook his head. He laughed again, silently but more intensely, huffing away to himself so strongly that for a while he could not speak. He slapped the table.

Charlie waited patiently. Geoff wiped a hand across his eyes. He stopped laughing, unsure whether his tears were really tears of laughter. His expression fell. He took the folded newspaper from his pocket and handed it to Charlie, who took only a minute to absorb the gist. He tossed the newspaper onto the table and took a sip of his tea.

"Microbes, eh?" Charlie said.

"Just when you think they can't think of anything else that deserves rights, they come up with something," said Geoff. He leaned over the table towards Charlie, who remained where he was, arms folded. "Where will it all end, that's what I want to know. Where?" Geoff said in a lowered tone.

Charlie eyed him through lowered lids but didn't reply. He stirred his tea and gazed out of the window.

"We fought for a better world," Geoff hissed. "Not this, this ...." He gestured vaguely around his head. "This."

Charlie shrugged. "It was what we all wanted back then. It was the right thing to do."

"Oh, come on. Don't spout the party line. The truth is we got more than we bargained for, and we lost a lot, too. But no one likes to admit it."

Charlie folded his arms.

Geoff leaned back in his chair. "I know, I know. It's just, this isn't how I'd imagined things would turn out, that's all."

He sighed and gazed around the cafe. The waitress was dissolving a cube of dry Syn tea in a jug of water. People wearing old, worn clothes sat at the tables. There was a quiet buzz of conversation.

From outside the cafe the sudden sound of dogs barking and growling broke through the soft hum of voices. The men looked out through the cafe window. A terrified child stood at bay, her back against the street wall, while a pack of strays surrounded her. One of the dogs darted forward and nipped the child's leg. She screamed.

"Bloody hell," said Geoff. "Bloody dogs." He jumped

out of his chair, knocking it over backwards.

"It's all right. Someone's on to it. Look," said Charlie.

A passerby, a tall man, had stepped between the dogs and the child, holding a long stick out in front of him. The child clung to the back of the man's coat, burying her face in the cloth. The man slowly backed away from the dogs, keeping the child behind him. Geoff picked up his chair and sat down again while the cafe patrons watched the events outside.

"I don't know," commented a woman wrapped in a shawl full of holes, sitting at the table nearest Geoff and Charlie. "Who lets a young child like that out on their own? Don't parents have any sense these days?"

"I know," said her friend. "Fancy being allowed to have a child, then letting it roam the streets? It's criminal. Her parents should be locked up."

"Some people don't realise how lucky they are. If parents can't take better care of their children, they should take the kids off them. Give them to someone who'll appreciate them, that's what I think."

"Too right," said the friend, nodding.

The women returned their attention to the scene. The man and child were farther down the street and the dogs were starting to lose interest.

"He didn't hurt the dogs, did he?" said the woman in the shawl.

"No. Silly girl must have done something to provoke them," her friend said.

"Yeah, kids never learn, do they?"

Geoff ground his teeth.

"If my wife and I had been allowed to have kids, I would've whacked any dog that came near them," he spat at the women.

Open-mouthed, they stared at him without response. His comment had been loud enough to be heard by others sitting nearby, who also turned to Geoff with looks of alarm.

"Now then, Geoff," said Charlie. He reached out to pat his friend's arm, but Geoff snatched it away and stood up. He turned to the cafe patrons.

"Dogs before children? You're mad, all of you. Insane."

"Geoff." Charlie stood up.

"I'm off. I've had enough of this," said Geoff, and strode to the cafe door.

"Oy, wait a minute," said Charlie, hurrying after him.

Geoff paused. "What?"

"Outside," said Charlie. The cafe customers had not lost their interest in Geoff and were watching curiously.

Charlie closed the door behind him. He took Geoff by the arm and marched him a few steps before stopping and turning to face his friend.

"I've been meaning to say something for a while," said Charlie. "I don't know exactly how to put this, but, I think you should be more careful."

"What do you mean?"

Charlie looked both embarrassed and annoyed.

"You know what I mean."

Geoff felt a tingle of fear.

"I don't think I ..."

"Look, I can smell them on you. And if I can, others can too."

Geoff scrambled for a reply. "What? How do you ...?"

"My father used to be a grower. Back when it was legal. And look at your hands, you idiot."

Geoff looked down and turned his hands palm upwards. They were covered in green smudges from where he had been examining his plants. Cold fear crept over him. He had had no idea it was so obvious.

"But I'm not harming anyone, or anything, Charlie. I'm giving things life. What can be wrong with that? I'm not doing any harm. You understand, surely?"

Charlie's only reply was a hard-faced stare.

"I mean, thanks. For the warning," said Geoff.

"It's only because you're an old friend. I don't approve. And I'd appreciate it if you kept your distance while you're at it. I don't want anyone getting the impression I've got anything to do with your activities." He leaned close to Geoff's ear.

"Where do you think the electric's coming from for your little operation? And the water?" He shook his head. "It's easy, mate. Tread lightly. It's all we have to do." Charlie didn't wait for a reply, but turned and walked away without looking back.

On his way home, the trembling and sweating Geoff had experienced that morning returned. He had only wanted a little bit of variety in his diet. Selling the extra was just a sideline. Syn strips, Syn soup, Syn tea, they got boring after a while. But Charlie's revelation filled him with fear.

He turned the corner into his street, which was almost empty, with just a few other walkers navigating the cracked, uneven, pavement, grass and weeds. Geoff saw the quick flash of a rat's tail disappearing down a drain. How had putting a stop to cruelty, ignorance and destruction turned into this? He felt stooped and old, too old to figure it all out.

He resolved to dismantle his growing set-up as soon as he got home. He could let the plants rot in his attic and no one would ever find out. He had had his fun, but now it was time to be sensible. His small pleasure was not worth dying for, and he did not want to spend his final years living in fear. He would just have to accept things the way they were. His intentions filled him with relief and he began strolling happily.

Opening his front door, Geoff could smell the green smell from the plants in his attic. In his relaxed state, it took a moment for the realisation of what this meant to hit him. A moment too long for him to even try to run. As he stepped into his home, a hand grabbed him roughly and slammed him against his hallway wall, cracking his head. He attempted a muffled, dazed protest but the hand was unforgiving, pinning him against the wall by the scruff of his neck.

"Geoffrey Finch?" said a woman's voice at his side.

Geoff tried to nod.

"Turn him round," instructed the voice.

Geoff found himself spun round by his shoulder. He staggered as the hold on him was released. He felt blood trickle from a cut on his forehead.

"You are Geoffrey Finch?"

"I, er," Geoff looked at the people standing in his hallway. Five police officers. Geoff's heart sank. "I ..." He could not speak. He nodded.

The woman in charge held up four tomatoes for him to see. They were red, ripe, and smelled delicious.

"You grew these?"

Geoff could see no point in denying it. He nodded again, a tear trickling down his face.

***

There was no trial. Geoff admitted his guilt. It was a foregone conclusion, and when he thought it over he realised was tired of life anyway. He did not recognise the world he lived in anymore, and he could not understand where or why exactly everything had changed.

He had only a week to wait. He spent the entire time in his cell, his face turned towards the wall.

At last the guards came for him. They took him to a small room containing a hospital bed, a doctor and two nurses. Geoff noticed the restraints on the bed.

He spoke the thought at the forefront of his mind.

"Will it be quick?"

"Quick? In what sense?" The doctor stopped checking the various hypodermics on a tray and regarded him, puzzled.

"I mean, will it be over quickly? I don't mind dying, but I'd rather get it over with, you know."

A look passed between the medical personnel and the guards. No one seemed keen to answer the question. Finally the doctor took it upon herself to break the news.

"Mr. Finch, you aren't going to die."

An expression of joy filled Geoff's face. He started forward and turned, staring at the others in the room, but none would make eye contact. The guards readied the batons in their hands. Geoff's face fell into a confused frown.

"But my crime carries the death penalty."

"You *have* lost your right to life."

"So, do I just get life imprisonment or something?"

"I'm afraid you misunderstand. *You* have lost your right to life. But your body is host to billions of microbes. They haven't lost their right to life. If we kill you, we kill them too." Geoff turned white. The doctor mouthed 'chair' to a nurse, who deftly inserted one beneath him as his knees buckled.

"Wh ... what does this mean?"

"It means, Mr. Finch, that your body will be kept here, alive, confined to this bed. We will continue to support your bodily functions until you die a natural death."

Geoff turned cold. He tried to mouth some words but nothing came out. The doctor signalled to the guards, who lifted Geoff from the chair and strapped him to the bed.

He stared up at the ceiling. The doctor's face appeared in his field of vision.

"The sentencing judge has granted you an Act of Mercy, though. You can choose to be conscious or unconscious during the process."

But Geoff couldn't find words to reply.

"Conscious or unconscious? Mr. Finch? Mr. Finch?"

Robot Relations

Cynthia had a problem with Gus from the very first day he arrived at her office. The management made a big show of introducing their new 'employee'. Calling the entire office into a mid-afternoon meeting, the CEO himself showed up to announce that their department was lucky enough to participate in an experiment in human/android work relations. Whereas previously humans and androids had worked in segregated environments, it was clear to business leaders that in an increasingly competitive global market, it was necessary and desirable that there should be greater integration in order to maximise efficiency and therefore profits. Not only that, now that there had been huge strides made in safety protocols, earlier concerns over potential dangers in the practice were no longer pertinent. A few of the staff had stirred uneasily at this, apparently unconvinced by his hearty words.

And then Gus was brought in. He seemed normal enough. He looked like an ordinary, fairly short man with light brown, collar length hair cut sharply away from his face in the new style. Invited to say a few words, all he managed was,

"Hi everyone. I look forward to working with you and I'm sure we'll all manage to get along just fine."

That was it. The next day Gus turned up for work the same as everyone else.

A few months passed without incident and Gus seemed to be fitting in pretty well, but Cynthia just couldn't seem to work or communicate with him without feeling silly, even though he could speak quite well and complete the tasks he was given (albeit slowly, it had to be said). It felt strange having Gus in the office working alongside everyone else as if it were the most normal thing in the world. She understood that this was the way things were going now; that this was progress, the future, so to speak, and that it was pointless trying to buck the trend or put up a fight about it. She had also read about the push from the Government for companies to diversify their workforces, and she knew that with a booming economy and a labour shortage it was inevitable that this would happen.

That was her intellectual understanding, however. When confronted with the material evidence of it in her office, she found she reacted on another, deeper level.

Such work difficulties would not normally have bothered her much. After all, you could not expect to get along with everyone or every*thing* you worked with. But her co-workers seemed to have such a good relationship with Gus that her failure to accept him made her question whether there was something wrong with her; whether she was quite normal.

He was seated at the first cubicle you came to when you entered the office, and everyone else would say hi to him when they arrived for work. When a funny email circulated, his address was included in the list. If there was ever a work excursion organised, Gus was always invited along, too. These were the kind of things that really disconcerted and puzzled her. She could understand that it was necessary to treat Gus like any other member of the workforce on a professional level; that he had to be included in everything work-related; and that he had the same entitlements as everyone else. The anti-discrimination legislation mandated all that. But social interaction? Social events? How did that make any sense?

Cynthia coped with the situation as best she could. She devised a number of strategies for the start of the working day. The expectation that she should offer a greeting made her feel awkward, so, when entering the office, she would move quickly past Gus and not look in his direction. Sometimes she would hang around in the lobby, waiting for another colleague to accompany her past Gus' desk, and she would not pause her half of the dialogue while the colleague uttered a brief 'Hey, Gus'.

Other times she would take something from her case in the lift on the way up to her floor, and pretend to be reading it as she entered the workplace. Mostly she would go into the kind of reverie people enter on a crowded underground train, there but not quite there, staring into middle distance to avoid acknowledging the presence of the other commuters. Similar strategies were employed on her way out. As for staff excursions, she did not generally go on those anyway, so it was easy to avoid one if she knew Gus was going. Consequently what he did on them and how the rest of the staff dealt with his presence was a mystery to her.

Day to day work-related interactions were easier. They had little contact, and she found she could treat Gus similar to a co-worker if she was focusing on the work itself, the reason both he and she were there, essentially. She could exchange information or updates with him, instruct him to perform tasks, even speak with him if the conversation were necessary and factual. He was there to do a job and so was she. As a professional, she was fairly comfortable with that. He was useful in his own way, and competent enough to fulfil his role. In that way, she found she could appreciate his efforts as she would those of any other colleague. But the informal relationship that the other staff had struck up with him eluded her.

There was no doubt the fault was entirely her own. Gus had been equally friendly towards her as he was towards the other members of staff, if not more so. Perhaps he had sensed her discomfort and was trying to put her at ease? She did not know. He had, on more than one occasion, tried to steer a professional discussion into a less formal one, but each time she avoided his attempts. She took her work very seriously so it was not difficult for her to do this, but she was especially on guard with Gus.

Cyythia wondered whether the others noticed. No one had commented on it, but she had the suspicion that whenever there was a brief glance in her direction, or some quiet chatter and laughter as a co-worker lingered at another's cubicle, or when she noticed someone minimising the work on their screen as she entered an office, that it was all about her, about her inability to deal with the new staff member. Was she being paranoid? She did not know. She was not so insecure that she needed others' approval, but she was well aware of office gossip and the detrimental effect it could have on one's career. If the others really were talking about her, if they thought she could not handle having Gus in the office, how would that be seen by the upper management? She did not know for sure, but it probably wouldn't count in her favour. How to address the problem, though? She could not help her reaction to him. She thought *she* was the normal one.

Did Gus notice that she treated him differently? That was another concern. If he did, he had not made a formal complaint as she would have heard about it soon enough. Other than that, Cynthia had no way of telling. She had had no training at all in interpreting their behaviour, though she was sure such programmes must exist. She had been unable to develop an understanding as the others had apparently done. His face formed expressions and his voice had intonation, but she could not read or interpret either of them at all.

Luckily for Cynthia, her cubicle was located at the back of the office, so most days she only saw Gus four times, on her way in and out, to and from home, and at lunch time. Lately though, she had been encountering him more and more often. Whenever she had cause to leave her desk, he always seemed be up and around at the same time and in the same place, unavoidable. And he always wanted to start a conversation.

"Hey, it's Cynthia, right? We don't see much of each other, do we? With me working at at the front and you hiding all the way back here in your little cubbyhole."

It was hard for her to know what to say in these situations where they could be overheard. She did not want to seem standoffish. If she already had a reputation for being prejudiced that would only make it worse. On the other hand, what was she supposed to say? She tried her best to act normal.

"Ha ha, no, you're right, " would be the kind of inane reply she would make.

She knew she should say more, add something like, *it's Gus, isn't it*? but she could not bring herself to. She would pretend to be in a hurry and dash past him, hoping no one would think her behaviour odd.

But Gus was persistent. The 'chance' encounters increased in frequency until one day he finally got up his courage to take their acquaintance a step further. As she left for a break, Cynthia found him standing right outside her cubicle. She almost bumped into him. He planted himself firmly in front of her, so that she would have to go around him to escape. He had a look on his face. Determined? Cynthia found the expression as difficult to read as all the others.

"Hi Cynthia, how are you?"

"Fine."

A pause.

"And you?"

"I'm good."

"Great, well, I'm just off on my break—"

"Yeah, me too, but I must tell you about something I was reading the other day. It'll really make you chuckle."

Not wanting to encourage him, but not wanting to appear rude either, Cynthia did not reply, but she also did notmove away. She was going to have to hear him out. He continued.

"Yeah, it was an article I was just quickly scanning. It was saying the weirdest thing. It'll make you laugh so much. It'll …." He seemed to become conscious of her silence. "It'll … ummm." He stopped, paused an unbearably long time, then his words poured forth in a torrent: "The article said that it was possible for there to be relationships between, between, you know, androids and, and, and errrr … humans. I don't mean just friends, I mean …." The torrent dwindled to a trickle.

Rocked to the core at what she had just heard, Cynthia marched past Gus, bowling him over as she left. What the others thought did not matter anymore. To stand there in the presence of that, that *thing* and listen to the abominable suggestion uttered from its mouth was more than she could bear. She raced out of the office. It was a long time before she could compose herself enough to go back to work.

Reflecting on the encounter later that day, she wished she ha had the presence of mind to deal with the situation properly, professionally; but she had been too shocked. She knew that Gus had fitted in pretty well at the office, that they had all got used to him and he to them, presumably, but she had had no idea that a feeling like *that* had formed in him, let alone about *her*.

She regretted the horror she must have shown as she speedily left his presence. That must have affected him. They had feelings, or so she had heard. But what was she supposed to do? How was she supposed to react to such an execrable proposition? She knew then that, risky though it was to her professional standing, she simply had to approach a higher level in the company before the situation got out of hand.

Later that day, when most of the staff had gone home, Cynthia spoke with one of the more accessible managers on the team in his office. Rather than tell him of her most recent encounter with Gus, she thought it safer that she voiced a general concern. After all, she would not want the situation to be interpreted incorrectly, nor for the story of the embarrassing encounter to be long associated with her carefully nurtured good name.

"But can I ask why we have to have one of them on our staff Mr. Grannen? Forgive me if I'm speaking out of turn but it isn't as if they're at all efficient. I can work at twice Gus' pace, I'm sure. And what else does he bring to the workplace? Sure, everyone's polite. I'm mean no one's *said* anything, and I'm sure they wouldn't. It wouldn't be right, I know, to discriminate or anything like that. I know they have rights, and I'm not saying they shouldn't but ...."

Cynthia had worked in business long enough to know when she had started to dig herself a nice hole, and she had developed enough good sense to know when to stop. Grannen's mouth creased into a small smile. He filled the awkward silence.

"Cynthia, Gus is an asset to this company in many ways. He's personable, friendly, a good team player." Seeing the look on Cynthia's face, he paused.

"Okay. I'll level with you, but this isn't to get back to the others, okay?"

She nodded and leaned in. He lowered his voice. "Look, I don't know how best to put this without sounding ... you know," he faltered.

"I know just what you mean, Mr Grannen."

He continued quietly, "Cynthia, Gus is, well, he's a gimmick." He raised his voice slightly. "I don't mean to denigrate him in any way, of course."

"Oh, of course!"

"He has lots to offer the company."

"Yes!"

"But mostly he's here because the customers like him. They like the novelty when they come in and see him sitting there ... working away." They chuckled conspiratorially.

Grannen leaned back and smiled. "Cut him some slack, Cynthia. It isn't easy to for new personnel to fit in, and of course it's going to be especially hard for Gus. What is it they're always saying to each other?" He considered for a moment, then started laughing again as he remembered the phrase he was searching for. "Yeah, that's it! He's only human, after all!"

Cynthia sighed. Shoulders slumped, she returned to her cubicle. As she passed Gus' desk, he looked up, and winked. Cynthia averted her gaze, barely repressed a shudder, and went back to her work.

What Poppa Pills Did For Me

The New New York Times Wednesday, October 11, 2193

OBITUARIES: Elizabeth Brown, Longest-Lived Person in the History of Humankind, Dies at 211

Elizabeth Brown, record holder for the longest documented human lifespan, died today at Bethlehem End-of-Life Centre, London. She was 211 years, 6 months and 9 days old when her life-support was turned off. Ms. Brown beats the previous record holder, Yasoshomi Yuguri, by 3 months and 17 days. Ms. Yuguri had held the record for more than two years before Ms. Brown came along and smashed it.

Elizabeth Brown published several guides to living longer. Her advice included eating plenty of high quality dark chocolate and maintaining good mental health by living an easy and stress-free life. Of course, it helped to be a member of a family worth trillions of pounds in stock, real estate and corporations.

There was celebration in the streets of the capital this evening after the news was announced by Ms. Brown's daughter, Natasha, who is herself a sprightly 185 years old.

"Toward the end, Mother was adamant that she wanted to go," said Natasha at a press conference held shortly after the announcement was made. "As a family, we've made it our priority to use whatever means available to extend our lives. Mother had several operations over the years and made full use of whatever medical breakthroughs occurred. She'd had most of her major organs cloned and replaced, and I think she was on her third heart," Natasha said. "It was hard to keep track sometimes. But she finally decided enough was enough."

When asked what was her mother's motivation to try to live as long as possible, Ms. Brown said:

"Well, in my family we all just love living! We all have a real zest for life. We travel, we learn about new things all the time. My husband and I have just got back from a trip to Nova Scotia. We couldn't believe how much it had changed since we were there a century ago.

"But it isn't only that. We're a very patriotic family.

We like to do our bit for the country. When Yasoshimi Yuguri lived to 211, well, we thought, we can beat that easily. Britain might not have its empire anymore, but we can still show the rest of the world what we're made of."

Did Natasha have any advice to pass on for those who aren't in such a privileged position?

"I think the average person can do a lot to prolong their life these days," she said. "As well as taking Poppa-Pills — Mother told me she had been taking them religiously ever since they first came out — you should get regular checkups to get any cancers sorted out immediately, and keep your brain working. All these things do a lot to increase your lifespan. Take my family—please! No, seriously, we're learning new things all the time. I can speak four languages and I've just started on Mandarin."

"Of course, there still aren't any brain transplants available; otherwise Mother would have gone for one like a shot!" said Natasha. "That's what forced her hand in the end. She didn't want to risk any loss of her mental faculties."

Elizabeth Brown had been increasingly concerned about the quality of her brain function, although she was fully compos mentis when she died, according to her medical team at the hospital.

Thoughts now turn to the next in line to break Ms. Brown's record. There are a number of contenders in both Asia and the United States, most notably Agatha Williams of Texas and Ping Yee-Ling of Hong Kong, both of whom are within one year of Ms. Browns' record age.

For the time being, however, the record stays with Britain. Elizabeth Brown's state funeral will be held at Westminster Abbey this Friday.

King Brian is expected to attend, as well as the Prime Minister and other heads of state. It is expected to be a joyous affair, celebrating Ms. Brown's long life. Her entire immediate family, consisting of husband Michael (157), daughters Natasha (185) and Beverley (163), and grandson Phillip (101 and the last in the Brown line) will be seated with the dignitaries. Michael was Elizabeth Brown's third husband after being widowed twice.

Regarding the funeral arrangements, Natasha said that her mother was delighted to hear that she will receive full privileges, including a glass gun carriage to transport her body and a service led by the Archbishop of Canterbury, Vijay Singh.

"We'll also be holding a small family gathering afterwards," said Natasha, "just for close relatives and friends. We'd like to remember mother's life in a personal way, too. After all, it isn't every day you have a record-breaker in the family!"

And Elizabeth herself?

"Oh, we'll make sure Mother's included in everything. She'll be watching the funeral through her interface, and once we're all home, we'll talk with her through the house system so she can join in the celebration too."

Asked why Elizabeth herself was not available for interview, Natasha said her mother was still getting used to cyberlife, but she was booked to take part in the Gene Getterby Show next Thursday, and she intended to honor that commitment.

Elizabeth Brown's book, *What Poppa Pills Did For Me*, will be out in Spring, 2194.

Why I Chose Him

Dear Abitha

If you're reading this letter it's because I'm gone.

I want to finally answer the question that's stood between us for so long. I'm sorry I never had the courage to explain, but you deserve to know why your brother had a chance to escape Earth and you didn't. I write this in the hope that you'll forgive me.

"The pussy is sweeter than the tit." That's what your Yaya said to me once, or I think she did. I never did learn much Greek. But it sounds like something a mother would say to her future daughter-in-law, don't you think? Certainly something Yaya would say to me. And whether it was really an old Greek saying like your dad said or just something Yaya made up, I don't know. But I can't deny her words crossed my mind when I was making my decision about which of you to send to a new life when the chance came.

Do you remember when we said goodbye to your brother? He looked so smart in his cadet's uniform, standing with the other colonists on the ramp of La Pinta. Eyes clear and bright, hair neater than it had ever been in his thirteen years of life. He looked incredibly brave and hopeful. And so young. As we hugged him so tight it must've hurt him, even then, there was a little voice telling me that I would only lose him to some girl, eventually, if he stayed.

"The pussy is sweeter than the tit." Yaya was right, I think. I hope. Better to let him take the chance and go and find that girl, make a life, on a new planet. Out of this hellhole.

There were other reasons. Some, I don't think I was even that aware of at the time. One of them struck me like a lightning bolt long after Kyrion left and your dad was long gone, too. You were working as a technician at the time. The climate was bad. Heat, dust storms. I can picture the moment perfectly as I write, even though it happened more than forty years ago.

I'm at home, waiting for you to come in from work. You unzip the entrance, and step through, scattering dust over the living room. You're thick with it. If I didn't know it was you I probably wouldn't recognise my own daughter. You walk through to the shower, and I clean up after you. Ten minutes later, you step out. You've sluiced off the dirt, washed your hair. You're standing there in your dressing gown, your light blue eyes vivid against your dark hair and skin. And you look at me. You don't mean anything by it, but you look at me with that gaze that seems to see right through everything, and the light catches your eyes, glints off your hair, and it's as much as I can do not to catch my breath. You are beautiful. You shine. And I can't believe I helped make this gorgeous creature.

It struck me then, one of the reasons I chose your brother. It was because I didn't want to be deprived of seeing my daughter grow into a woman. As your mother I wanted to be there, and share in that.

But I don't want you to think my decision was purely selfish. You probably don't remember but there was a form for people like me. The ones who'd had twins, so were left out of the lottery and, instead, had to choose a child to go, a child to stay. We were supposed to list your strengths and weaknesses, to help decide where your skills would be most useful, on a new colony or on our old, failing Earth.

You were into electronics even then, always pulling things apart and finding out how they worked, while Kyrion was born a farmer. He was never happy unless he had his hands in dirt. I knew if anyone could work the soil of an alien world and make it bear crops, he could. I knew he was needed there. And here, where finally we were trying to fix the harm we'd done, you were needed, to develop the technology to reverse the damage.

What could Kyrion have done here if he'd stayed? Do you remember him trying to grow beans in the yard? Three years he tried, in that rocky dust, and each year the shoots would wither and burn. Poor kid. I caught him sharing his water ration with those little doomed plants once, going thirsty to give them a chance.

Now that I'm dead, Abitha, I hope you'll continue to talk and listen to him. I know it's weird. He's still a teenager and we've grown old. It must be weird for him too, communicating with his twin who's now middle-aged. But remember that for him it's only a few years since he left. And now his mum is dead. So, please, for as long as you can, talk to him.

I've left the hardest thing to say till last. I'm sorry I deprived you of children of your own. When I was young the one child policy seemed to be working. I had no idea things would get so bad they would start to dictate who could have kids. I couldn't look you in the face the day you found out you hadn't been selected. You see, that was another reason I chose Kyrion to go. I wanted to help you through that joy of pregnancy and birth. Of raising your child. I was so selfish.

The fact was, I didn't choose your brother. I chose you. God help me, I chose you.

I love you

Mum

The Last Days of Duane Dayton

Duane's hands closed around Meryl's neck, stifling her screams to harsh, guttural choking. Her terrified eyes widened. Yes, this time he was really going to do it. She twisted and squirmed. She tore at his fingers, reached up to claw his face. But his arms were longer and he pulled his head out of harm's way. She dug her nails into the flesh of his hands and arms, but the pain only drove him on. Legs thrashing, she heaved and wrenched as her face turned purple and her eyes bulged. Her lungs fought to draw air. Gradually her efforts weakened and subsided. Duane felt her neck give as he crushed her voice box in his meaty grip. She scrabbled at his hands. Tears slid from her eyes, and they closed. Her body went limp. Duane maintained the vice around her throat, waiting for that moment when life departed. She slipped away. He eased his hands open and stood up, savoring the sight of the corpse at his feet.

And then he was back in his cell, sitting on the edge

of his bunk. He slumped onto it, tears overflowing his eyes. Each time it caught him by surprise. Each time the memory of the murder affected him worse. He plunged into darkness. He pounded his bunk with his fist again and again. Why did she always make him angry? Why did she make him do it? That bitch deserved everything she got.

Hours later, he found himself staring at the wall opposite, eight feet from his nose. It was bare, cream, featureless. On the wall was a shelf holding a single book. He was only allowed one at a time. *The Green Mile* was his selection for that day, a story of evil and good prisoners and bulls. He wished he was like John Coffey, the big black prisoner with magical powers, but feared he was more like Wild Bill Wharton, the evil son-of-a-bitch. Duane took the book down. He remembered seeing the film as a young child. Pops always let him watch whatever he wanted. Maybe if he read the book for the fiftieth time it would drive Meryl's death from his mind.

As he lay back his cell door opened and a man and woman walked in. Duane sat up. The woman he already knew. Sweet Ass. Tall and skinny but with a behind to make you weep, she could pass for something if she let down her ponytail and put on some makeup. The guy was paunchy. A neckbeard with zits. He looked familiar but Duane couldn't place him. Probably he had fixed the dude's car at the shop one time.

"It's pretty straightforward," the woman said "just shut him down, run a system check. If everything's working properly, no bugs, just start him up again."

The man chuckled uneasily, and glanced sideways towards Duane's bunk.

"Something wrong?" asked the woman.

"Just seems a bit weird, you talking about *him* like that."

"Yeah, well, technically he's still human. Still got a few rights. So you gotta take care, you know? Lose some data or something, you won't stay in this job long."

"Sure, sure, I'll be careful. It sounds simple enough, like you said—oh—" The man spoke out of the corner of his mouth, "Is he on? I mean ..." He glanced towards the bunk again. "Can he hear us?"

The woman walked over to Duane and looked into empty air. "Yep. Probably listening in right now. See this?" She pointed to nothing at all to the right of Duane's head. "Mic. Turn it off—" She pressed an invisible button. Duane saw the two figures continue to talk but heard only silence. The woman pressed the button again, and the voices returned. "And this?" said the woman. Her finger disappeared in Duane's shoulder. "Camera. And it's on, so he can see us. But if I turn it off ..." Everything turned pitch black. "He can't see a thing." A moment later light reappeared.

"Wow. Jeez." The man scratched his stubble. He stepped up to the woman's side and bent his head towards hers. "How come he ain't saying something?" he asked, his voice low.

"Speaker's off," said the woman. "And if you take my advice you won't turn it on. Talk about creepy," she said, with a shudder.

"Yeah, you don't wanna hear what I wanna do to you, darlin'," said Duane. The neckbeard and the woman talked about technical stuff, and Duane's eyes roved the woman's body, imagining tearing those jeans down over that tight ass, ripping open her t-shirt, twisting the little titties out of her bra, biting—. The cell door banged closed behind the man and woman as they left. "Shee-it." Duane threw himself onto his back and picked up the book again. He began to read, but his mind wandered back to the woman and the neckbeard. Two techies. It looked like Neckbeard was taking over from Sweet Ass. Goddamnit. He had looked forward to her visits, even if he did only see her enter, press a button he couldn't see, press it again and leave. She was something to think about at least, even though he couldn't jerk it anymore.

Duane tried to focus on his book, but it was no good. He wondered what the people entering his cell saw. A metal and plastic box? He had never seen a bodybox, a PCD—a Personhood Containment Device—this thing he was stored in. Lived in. Was it black? With a lead to plug into the wall? And inside the box: all that remained of Duane Dayton.

Was he even in a cell? He wasn't sure. The view from the camera seemed to show the same background as the rest of his cell, but who knew how those techies messed with what he could and could not see. How much of it was real? Was he real?

Like Meryl's murder, Duane found it hard to prevent the memory of his execution from invading his mind. His pulse began to race as he recalled the walk from his cell to the execution room. He had tried to act tough. He was not going to have anyone say Duane Dayton went to his death scared, but the truth was he had had trouble controlling his bowels on that last walk. The last walk he had taken in real life. He remembered them strapping him down. The look of glee on Meryl's mother's face. The ice-fire of the injection flooding his veins. They had said it would not hurt. Goddamned liars.

Then he had woken up here. In Dead Row. Like nothing had changed. Like his body was not dead and cremated, and he was not a bunch of electrical signals roaming wires in a box, Meryl's murder playing over and over in his head. Duane threw *The Green Mile* on the floor. He stomped on it, grinding in his heel so that the cover should rip and the pages tear. But the book absorbed the pressure like rubber. He snatched it up and tried to wrench out the pages, but they resisted his hands. He threw himself against the cell door and pounded it with his fists and feet and head. No matter how hard he hit he felt no pain. No wounds appeared, no blood flowed from cuts. He hollered, screamed, howled.

Duane was curled into a fetal position on the floor of his cell when a man in a suit came in. The man walked through the prone Duane and *The Green Mile*, and pulled over the cell's single chair to opposite Duane's bunk. He pressed the invisible speaker button and sat down.

"Mr. Dayton? It's Markham here. I've come to update you on your case."

Duane stayed on the floor.

"Mr. Dayton?" Markham waited. "Fine," he said after a few moments, "I'll ask the administrators to—"

"I'm here. I'm listening." Duane pushed himself to his feet and dropped onto his bunk in front of the lawyer. He sat where he could pretend he was making eye contact with the man.

"I'll come straight to the point, Mr. Dayton. Ms.

Butler's family argued very strongly against your reassignment in court today. They had prepared excellent victim impact reports."

"Excellent reports, huh? I thought you was on my side?"

"I'm sorry, but I don't want to mislead you. There's no changing the fact that the loss of Ms. Butler has caused significant emotional and material damage to the Butler children and the rest of the Butler family."

"They're Dayton kids. They're my kids!"

"Mr. Dayton, if you cannot control yourself I'll have to leave," said Markham.

"Then leave," roared Duane, but immediately checked himself. "No, stay. Stay." The lawyer would probably be the only person he would see for days. "I'm ... sorry."

Markham straightened the creases on his trousers. "Very well. But I actually don't have much more to report. Things are progressing, but slowly. We're investigating every possible avenue for appealing your conviction. There's still a small chance you may be released. You mustn't give up hope."

But the lawyer did not seem to believe his own words. There would be no cloned Duane body to be reassigned to. His conviction would be upheld, and one day, in a few months' or years' time, he would be turned off.

"How much longer do you think I've got in here?" said Duane, then he decided he did not want to know. "How are my kids doing?"

"As far as I'm aware they're doing well. I mean, as well as can be expected," said the lawyer, "in the circumstances."

A sting pierced Duane's heart. He imagined Dakota and Brandy being brought up by Meryl's family. Being told what a bad man their daddy was. And he was. He was.

"Ain't there nothing good you can tell me?" asked Duane. "Why are they keeping me hanging around like this? It ain't right. They shoulda finished it all when I was found guilty. This is just cruel."

For a moment Markham regarded his hands, which were folded on his lap. "Mr. Dayton, the conditions you experience in your current capacity shouldn't be very different from living on Death Row as it used to be. If your conviction is overturned you can look forward to a brand new body, free of the diseases of aging. In return the State Government is able to save a substantial portion of its budget—"

"I want it to end."

"Mr. Dayton, you're being very premature. There are still many legal avenues we have yet to—"

"Are you my lawyer or what?"

"I am charged with representing you, yes."

"Then you gotta do what I say."

"I have a professional duty to provide you with the best defence possible, Duane."

The man would be squirming in his seat if he was not so stuck up, thought Duane. "Naw. You gotta do what I say. And I'm sayin' I don't want no more appeals. I'm guilty as charged. I put my hands round that bitch's neck and I squeezed the life outta her. And goddamnit I'd do it again if someone drove me to it like she did. So I've had it. I want out."

Markham protested and reasoned, but Duane refused to answer. The lawyer turned off Duane's speaker before he left.

***

Duane looked around him. *The Green Mile* had disappeared from the cell floor. Another day. There was a new book on the shelf: *The Bird Man of Alcatraz*. Duane had seen the old black and white movie. Pops' favorite. Pops had loved the old timers' movies. It was about a prisoner in solitary confinement who catches a bird and makes it his pet. He fills his cell with birds in little cages he makes by himself, and learns all about birds and becomes an expert, better than all the other experts. He saves birds' lives from diseases with his special cures. Duane picked up the book and lay down on his bunk. Prisons were better places in the olden days, he reflected.

His cell door opened and the male techie walked in. Duane put down his book.

"What're you doing here?" he asked. Sweet Ass had run her last check on his bodybox just a few days ago. He could not understand why Neckbeard was back so soon. Duane caught a glimpse of a small, black object in his hand as the man pressed the button to shut the bodybox system down.

Being turned off and on again was like moving from one day to another—the blink of an eye. Duane didn't know how long he had been turned off or what the man had done, but suddenly Neckbeard was in a different position. His gut was right in front of Duane's face. The man bent down and peered into the space where Duane knew the bodybox camera to be, as if he wanted to look Duane in the eye. He leered and winked. Once more, Duane thought he knew the man from somewhere. Was he another regular at his bar? A neighbour? And what was that wink about?

The Gunslinger, To Kill a Mockingbird, Papillon, Midnight Express .... The days passed. Duane saw no one but Neckbeard, who he concluded must be entering his cell so often in preparation for the grand Turning Off. He wondered how they would do it. Would Neckbeard shut him down permanently one day, just like that? No. They would have to have a big ceremony about it. Invite all the Butlers and anyone else who hated his guts. So they could all gloat for a second time. At least his kids were too young to attend.

Duane did not wonder what death was like. He had died once already, and then a hundred times more when his bodybox flipped him from day to day, or when they shut him down to check the system. Death was nothing. It was outside the pages of his book.

Markham looked sad when he finally arrived with the news, and Duane surprised himself by feeling touched. He had never liked the lawyer and he was pretty sure the lawyer had never liked him, but he had done his job, and now it obviously pained him that Duane had come to the end of the road. There was to be no grand display after all, it turned out. Despite the act they put on, the State Government did not really see prisoners living in bodyboxes as real people, and it thought that simply erasing their data was an acceptable way of putting an end to what was left of them. Markham placed his hand in the air, resting it on Duane's bodybox, before he left.

Duane picked up his book. It was called *Crime and Punishment*. It was about a murderer, like him, only this guy was stupid enough to confess. Duane had not known when he chose the book that it would be the last one he would ever read.

They came to delete him when he was halfway through the book again. Two bulls and Neckbeard. At least he did not have to worry about his bowels this time. He saw the techie walking toward him.

***

There was a room. A dirty room filled with empty pizza boxes, beer cans, computer equipment and wires. Endless wires. Duane reeled. Where was he? He could not take it in. He did not believe in Heaven or Hell, but what else could this be? It looked like the inside of a trailer. Hell was a dirty trailer? He tried to get up, but he could not move. He tried to turn his head to look around, to look at himself, but his head was fixed. He could look nowhere but straight ahead, and could see nothing but what was directly in front of him.

A figure crossed his view. He recognized the paunch with the t-shirt pulled tight across it immediately. Neckbeard. The figure crossed twice more, and both times Duane reflexively tried to follow it, but his vision remained restricted to the scene before him. A face appeared, inches away. Duane tried to pull back, but the image remained as large, so Duane could see each blackhead, stubble hair and jagged red line in the eyes.

"Hey Duane," Neckbeard said. "You can talk. I turned the speaker on."

"Hey," said Duane. "You gonna tell me what's happening?"

The techie whooped. "It worked," he exclaimed. "I knew it. Goddamnit, Jerod, you're one goddamned smart son-of-a-bitch, even if I do say so myself. Oh, yeah."

A dim, delicate hope began to form in Duane. The techie pushed aside some trash and settled into the sofa opposite. He spread his legs comfortably and took a swig from a beer can.

"Hey, Mr. Duane Dayton. How're you feeling?"

Confused, Duane did not answer for a moment.

"It's okay, Duane. It's just you and me. No one's gonna whip you back in jail."

"I'm okay. You got me out of prison? But this is different. I can't move. And I can't see anything 'cept what's right ahead."

The man swallowed a mouthful of beer and belched. "Yeah, sorry about that. I ain't got one of those fancy bodyboxes you're used to. But where you are is good enough. Better, in fact."

"So, what you planning?" Duane's faint hope began to flicker.

The man laughed. "You don't know who I am, do you? I didn't think you'd remember me. You always was one helluva self-centred bastard, Duane. Ah, fuck you." He got up and reached toward Duane.

Empty blackness and silence fell, but Duane remained conscious. He waited to see what would happen. Nothing. He was blind and deaf. He could not move or feel. Duane panicked. He raked his memory. Who was that man? He had called himself Jerod. Jerod ... Jerod. Duane ran through all the people in his past. Drinking buddies, guys down the bowling alley, kids he grew up with. He could not remember a Jerod. Maybe he was a friend of someone he knew, or ...? Oh, God.

Jerod was there again. He staggered a little as made his way back to the sofa.

"Jerod, I—"

"Remember me now, boy? I thought a little time alone might help."

"Jerod, look man—"

"Say my name, Duane. Say my whole name. You owe her that. You owe all of us that."

"I'm sorry, Jerod, you—"

"Say my goddamned fucking name."

"Jerod Butler. Your name's Jerod Butler. But, look, Jerod, I didn't mean for it to happen. She just got me so mad, man. You know what women are like."

Jerod's face filled Duane's vision, distorted, flushed, lips leaking saliva.

"My cousin was the sweetest, most beautiful woman that ever lived, Duane Dayton. And while the Lord may forgive your sins I sure as hell don't. So I made my own Hell for you right here. Dead Row Duane might be erased, but I copied every bit of you, and now here you are. And here you're gonna stay. Maybe I'll turn on your camera and mic one day—if I'm interested in how crazy you're getting in there. But I got a busy life, so don't expect to see too much of me."

Jerod stood up, so that Duane could see nothing but the man's belly. The last thing he heard was,

"Good night, Duane."

Breathing Space

Collins exhaled, inched himself forward a foot or so, then rested. He took shallow breaths. The narrowness of the rock tunnel would not allow anything more. His headlamp lit the way ahead. The rough limestone opened out in another four or five feet. His left arm lay stretched out in front of him, his right was trapped by his side. Collins' neck hurt from holding his head up, so he let it fall to the tunnel floor. Loose shards of rock pricked his cheeks, but the pain was preferable to the ache of his neck. Now, all his headlamp illuminated was the wall of the tunnel, a few inches from his eyes.

"How you doing? Much further?" Logan's voice came from somewhere beyond his feet, sounding as though he was far distant.

"Another few feet." Collins' words were instantly damped by the tunnel walls. He exhaled, and puffed dust from the floor into his eyes. They watered. He blinked. He could not reach them to wipe the dust away, not even with his free left arm. He blinked again, clearing the blur as best he could. He exhaled again, gentler this time, and inched his body further forward.

Pain from aching muscles and scraped, sore knees, hips, shoulders and elbows suffused through him, but as he lay there, thinking about the thousands of feet of rock and earth above and below, Collins could not resist a grin. The first few times he had done this, he had sweated in fear, unable to clear his mind of the image of himself permanently trapped, slowly dying of thirst and exposure, never to see sunlight nor feel fresh air on his skin again. Now, seasoned spelunker that he was, he relished the challenge.

"See anything yet? " Logan's faint voice crept into his ears.

"No ... just ... no. Nothing."

He could see discolouration on the tunnel wall a little way ahead. But rock coloring is always irregular. It could be anything.

Logan's question brought him back to the present and his mood sank a little. Was this the kind of place that Tedeschi had died? Had he tried a little too hard? Gone just a little further than was safe, and got stuck? Unable to move forward or back. Jammed solid, and alone. Until his lamp battery died and he was left in darkness so complete you could not see your hand before your face. Did he try calling out, even though the rock enclosing him deadened his loudest shout to a whisper? Did he scratch his fingers to the bone, hopelessly trying to dig through solid rock with his bare hands? Collins shivered and shook the images from his mind.

Exhale. Ease forward. Exhale. Ease again. The tunnel did not seem to narrow any further. He had enough room to breathe, just. A few more feet and he would be into the opening ahead, which looked big enough to sit up in and take a rest.

"Can't see you anymore."

"Must be about 20 feet, then."

"Would I fit?"

"Probably not. It's pretty tight in here." There was no way Logan would fit. Not that he was out of shape or anything. Just beefy. Great for drilling out rock or shifting it, hauling gear, but not the best body for a dedicated spelunker. Collins was grateful for his own wiry frame.

"Dang it. I can't never fit anywhere. Worst goddamn caver ever." Collins could see Logan in his mind's eye, leaning into the tunnel to talk to him, his doughy face wearing that dumb look he got whenever he tried to think too much.

"Why'd I even come along? No use to anyone. ... I should do something else, you know," Logan's faint monologue drifted through the tunnel. "There's gotta be a lot jobs for a guy like me. Mountain rescue, EMT..."

"Yeah, sure, Logan. You're scared of heights and you faint at the sight of blood. Now shut up, I'm nearly through."

Collins' head was level with the discoloured rock. Strange. It seemed to smell a little ... off. His left hand brushed the surface as he eased by. It did not feel any different. But the smell ... he could not place it. It was like nothing he had ever smelled before.

Then at last he reached the spot where the tunnel widened. Easing his aching muscles, he sat up. His neck and head were still forced down by the tunnel roof, but the space felt like luxury. After taking a breather, he bent down his head to get a closer look at the next section. A wider hole, then what looked like a chamber. He let out a whoop.

"What can you see?"

"It opens out. Room size."

"Anything there?"

Collins checked. "Can't see anything."

Freshened with excitement at his discovery of the new area, Collins wormed quickly through the remaining short tunnel and stood up. He stretched his shoulders back pleasurably and shook out his legs. Swinging his headlamp around, he examined the chamber. More discoloured rock, two or three tall, narrow openings that led deeper into the cave, and ... nothing. No sign of Tedeschi. No sign anyone had ever been here. Collins was most likely the first human ever to set foot in the place.

He peered into each opening in turn, then leaned down to call into the tunnel he had entered through.

"No sign he came this way."

"Dang it."

"There's three ways here. I guess I should call it a day."

"Guess so. It's getting late anyway. Time to head back."

Safety rules required spelunkers to stick together, never to go off alone. He could tell Logan which passage he was taking, but if he had an accident further on, would Logan remember? And if there was another choice of ways soon after, things would get confused.

Ignoring safety rules was what killed Tedeschi. Collins satisfied himself with a long look through each of the openings. They all led tantalizingly down. The recovery team had already gone as deep as the research team Tedeschi had belonged to, the deepest humans had ever been. This route he and Logan had found would break all the records.

After a regretful last look round, Collins squatted down to return the way he had come.

***

At base camp that night they watched the recordings from the expedition five weeks previously, when Tedeschi had disappeared. There he was, familiar to them all now. A small man. A good size for a caver. Lean but fit, carrying a ton of gear without it seeming much effort. No amateur. He moved over the rock at a measured pace, wasting no energy.

They watched him disappear into a sump, then fast-forwarded the recording to the point when he reappeared, grinning, giving a thumbs up, a sign he had found a way through. The delight on his face was what killed Collins a little. He knew that feeling. All the recovery team did. Tedeschi was one of them. He had come here for the same reasons they were all here. The same reasons they did the crazily dangerous things they loved to do. And now he was dead. Somewhere down here his body was lying in the dark.

As they were watching they heard the sound of more cavers arriving. Their team leader, Marsh, paused the video and turned to the watchers.

"It sounds like our guests are here. I know it goes against protocol, but we've a member of Tedeschi's team joining us. Dr. Surtees is a leading speleobiologist. She might be able to shed some light on conditions that influenced Tedeschi's disappearance."

Collins and Logan exchanged puzzled looks. Tedeschi had taken off alone and got stuck or lost. There was not any need to look for more causes than that. Caving was damned dangerous. People who did not follow the rules died. Sometimes they died even when they did follow the rules.

A tall woman stepped into the lamplight, begrimed from the journey down to the base camp. She dropped her pack heavily to the floor and sat down on it, resting her elbows on her knees. Her face was shadowed and lined. She nodded and smiled wanly at the recovery team members. A man from the group that accompanied her also stepped forward.

"We'll rest tonight and set off in the morning. Dr. Surtees has brought supplies for herself."

"We've plenty to spare, Dr. Surtees. Please help yourself if you need anything. There's some flat ground toward the back to set up camp. I guess you already know that," said Marsh.

Dr. Surtees did not reply. She was gazing at the frozen image on the screen. Tedeschi smiling into the camera, giving a thumbs-up.

After an awkward pause Marsh said, "Well, I'm sure you all know how to make yourselves at home." He started the recording again and the new arrivals walked off to find an area to settle for the night. Dr. Surtees stayed where she was.

Collins studied her instead of the recording. He had watched it so many times, he did not think there was anything else to learn, but the woman was something new. She had been there when Tedeschi went missing and would have been part of the first search, when they still had some chance of finding him alive. That must have been pretty harrowing. Yet here she was again, after what must only have been a few days topside. He could not read her expression. What had motivated her to return to look for the body?

When the recording had finished and they were wrapping things up, Collins decided he would try to find out. He held up a hand.

"I was wondering if Dr. Surtees would like to say anything? Can she tell us anything that might help us locate Tedeschi's body?"

She turned to look at him slowly, as if coming out of trance.

"I'm not sure," she said. "I think you probably already know everything I could tell you. Ted went missing two days after we made our final camp right here. We sent for help and searched for three weeks. Then it was decided there was no chance of finding him alive and we were recalled to the surface. We searched as far and as deep as we could, but you guys know the geology down here. It's a labyrinth."

"How about his state of mind? What do you think made him go off like that? He was experienced. It was a little odd, don't you think? Was he acting out of character?"

A guarded look passed over Dr. Surtees' face.

"No one knows why Ted took off. We couldn't figure it out. We woke up one morning and he was gone. As far as we could tell he hadn't taken more than basic equipment with him. You know this already, I'm sure."

She stood up and hauled her pack onto her shoulder. "Look, I'm sorry. I'm really tired." She walked away.

Collins turned to Logan and raised his eyebrows.

Logan shrugged. "She's tired. It's a long way from topside."

"We're all tired," replied Collins. "But why is she even here?"

"Why are any of us here? What's the point? That guy's long dead, and he's buried deeper and sleeping sounder than anyone else will be, ever."

"Don't start getting philosophical on me, Logan. We're here to do a job. If it was me I wouldn't want to be left alone here, dead or not. We should do our best to find Tedeschi and take him home. That woman was here when he disappeared. Maybe she can tell us something useful, even if she doesn't think she can."

Logan yawned. "Ask her tomorrow. Take her along with us if you like. I've never met a cave biologist. I bet she's got some good stories to tell."

"Maybe. Not about here, though. There's nothing alive down here but us as far as I've seen. But, yeah, I'll see if she'll join our team."

***

In the morning, Logan groaned as Collins shook him awake.

"Shut up, it's still early," Collins whispered.

"Jesus, let me sleep, man. What's the time?"

"Wake up, I want you to come with me. Hurry up."

Logan sat up and ran his hands through his hair. "What's the matter?" He put on his hard hat.

Collins leaned forward to speak into his ear. "I just saw that Surtees woman leave. Christ, you stink."

"Yeah, well, you're no eau de cologne yourself. She got up and left by herself? Which way?"

Collins pointed to one of the many passages leading from the large cavern they were camped in, just visible in the twilight of the dimmed camp lights.

"We're following her, right?" Logan had pulled himself out of his sleeping bag and was tying the laces on his boots.

Collins nodded. "If we wake the camp or wait we'll lose the element of surprise."

Logan grinned. "Been reading Sherlock Holmes again?"

"Shhh."

Stepping carefully around sleeping bodies the two made their way to the passage entrance. Turning their headlamps to the lowest setting, they began to walk quietly down the passage. After half a minute Collins stopped and whispered in Logan's ear.

"I'm going to turn off my lamp. You hang back aways

and I'll walk in the light from yours, okay?"

Logan nodded.

In light that it would have been impossible to see in after a few days topside, Collins stepped quietly and gingerly forward, holding his hands out in front of him. The passage rose gently. There was no floor, just rough stone, so both men had to frequently grip the walls to keep their balance. In places the passage narrowed to such an extent they had to turn sideways to pass through.

The feeble light from Logan's headlamp threw shadows from jagged rock formations, which jiggled and rose and fell as he walked. Collins strained his eyes to make out where to put his next step, and to check for light from Dr. Surtees' lamp ahead. Suddenly, the light from Logan's headlamp surged as he rushed forward. Collins felt Logan grab his shoulder and he turned to find out what the problem was. Logan put his finger to his lips. Then he heard it, too, so clearly he did not know why he had not heard it before. Tap, tap, tap. Collins had heard that sound so often it was unmistakable, a hammer and chisel on stone. But as soon as he recognised it, the sound stopped. Collins and Logan looked each other in the eyes. Had she heard them approaching? There was nothing for it but to continue on.

Still struggling to make his way in the puny light from

Logan's lamp, Collins half walked, half climbed forward, wincing inwardly at the slightest sound from his boots on the rock. He strained his eyes trying to see a glow in the darkness ahead, but there was nothing.

After another two or three minutes, his right boot trod on something soft. A small grunt issued from the object.

"Dr. Surtees?" Collins stepped back, bumping into Logan as he came up from behind. The black shape he had mistaken for a rock unfurled itself and elongated to human height. Collins and Logan turned their lamps on full, and Dr. Surtees did the same. Even in lamplight, her face shone red. Collins glanced down and saw her holding a plastic sample bag and hammer and chisel. The three stood in silence a moment, then the woman turned up her chin and gazed into Collins' eyes.

"You're the nosy one from last night, aren't you?"

"Hey, I'm just trying to find someone's remains. Not sure what you're doing here, though."

The woman tensed and drew herself up, then her face relaxed a moment and her eyes shone wet. She looked away and when she turned back she had resumed her fixed, unreadable expression. She lifted the sample bag and tools.

"I just wanted to collect some samples. It was stupid

of me to hide like that. I don't know why I did. Let's go back to the camp."

She tried to pass the two men, but it was not easy in a passage barely wide enough for one person, especially when the men clearly were not going anywhere.

"Tedeschi went off by himself, and died. Now you go off alone, too. Knowing full well what happened to your team mate. For samples? You could collect them anytime. And you said you were here to help the search," Collins said.

"I ... it's just ... these rocks." Surtees hesitated. "It's too hard to explain." She forced her way roughly passed Collins and Logan, and set off down the passageway.

Logan was just recovering from being thrust into the wall once when Collins pushed him aside again as he rushed after Surtees. He grabbed her shoulder and spun her round.

"Look, ma'am, this isn't good enough. We're down here risking our lives to try and find the body of your team mate, and here you go breaking safety rules again. What the hell? You want us to have two bodies to find down here? You want to end up like Tedeschi? Lying in the dark, alone, maybe hurt, dying of thirst? You think that's a good way to die?"

As he spoke, the guarded look fell from Surtees' face

and she collapsed to the floor, head in hands, sobbing.

"Don't ... please stop ... please." Her voice was muffled by her hands.

Collins stood over her, his hands on his hips. He threw a bemused, exasperated look at Logan, who seemed as confused as he was.

"Dammit, lady, what is it with you?" He stood indecisively for a moment, then reached down and grabbed Surtees' shoulders, lifting her to her feet.

"Let's just forget about all this, okay? We've found you now, so we'll go back to camp and start over, alright?"

Without answering, head down, Surtees started off down the passage, gripping the walls for support. Collins was about to follow when he noticed that she had left her sample bag on the floor where she had collapsed.

"Hey." He picked it up.

Surtees turned and saw what he was holding. She rushed back and snatched the bag from his hand, then stumbled away again. Collins and Logan followed, a little more slowly, so that a gap opened between the pair of them and Surtees. Collins felt Logan poke him in the back. He turned his head.

"What?"

"You made the cave biologist cry."

Collins rolled his eyes and continued scrambling through the passage.

***

Exhale. Inch forward. Stop to breathe. Exhale. Another few inches. Collins could not decide if it was his toes or his hips or his stomach that propelled him forward. Right arm lying ahead of him, left arm pressed against his side. Headlamp lighting the tunnel ahead. He was nearing the discoloured rock again.

Behind him, Logan and Surtees were watching the slow progress of his feet receding from them, waiting for him to reach the further chamber. The woman and her strange behaviour occupied Collins' thoughts. Back at camp, he had pressed her again, more gently this time, to explain herself, but she remained closed-lipped. Changing the subject, Logan had asked her about the samples she was collecting. She was not much more forthcoming, only mumbling something about they had looked interesting in the lab. When Collins had remarked they looked the same as another patch of rock he had seen the day before, she got very excited and asked to go with them to see it.

So here he was again. Once he was through, Surtees

would follow. As a pair, they could explore some of the passages leading from the chamber. On the way back, Surtees could take rock samples.

Collins' face eased passed the discoloured patch, inches from the surface. The smell seemed stronger today, and the rock glistened slightly in the beam from his headlamp. Such strange stuff. Collins was sure he had never come across this kind of rock before. But then, he was more than 9,000 feet below ground. Who knew what might be down here?

He looked ahead. The tunnel walls seemed narrower than before, which could not be possible. There were no cracks from shifted rock. Yet ... it looked so narrow, impossibly narrow. How could he fit through? If the tunnel really was as narrow as it seemed, how had he managed to get this far? Would he ever get out again? The edge of panic needled him. He pushed the feeling away, willing himself to breathe deeply to calm himself. But he could not breathe deeply. He was too tightly jammed, his chest barely fitting within the available space. He felt sweat break out on his face. His lungs worked against the constricting force of the tunnel walls. He heard himself begin to pant.

"Collins? ... Collins ..." He heard Logan's voice but he was concentrating on forcing down a rising tide of fear.

"What's wrong? Are you okay? What are you doing? What's happening? Collins?"

Instead of Logan's voice Collins heard, as if far distant, his own panting, rising in tone. A scream began to work its way up his throat. His body seemed to take on a life of its own, and struggled fruitlessly against the rock that enclosed him. He could hear his hard hat and boots thumping against the tunnel walls.

"COLLINS." Logan's shout broke through his mental turmoil. "What's happening? You okay, man?"

"Collins." Now it was Surtees. "Collins, move. Move forward. Just keep on going. Move."

He screwed his eyes shut, summoned up the little control he had left, and inched forward. And again. And again. His fear seemed to subside a little. He opened his eyes and saw the resting space ahead. Focusing on it, he eased another few inches. His panic fell away.

"Oh, Jesus." He slumped into the floor of the tunnel.

"Collins? Are you alright?" Logan called.

"Yeah ... yeah, I'm okay. I don't know what happened. I'm okay now."

Collins could not understand what had come over him. He had not ever panicked like that before. Was he losing it? If word of his panic attack got back to Marsh, he would kick him out for sure, for their and his own safety. Would Surtees report what had happened?

Probably. Logan was an old friend but he might, too, out of concern. Better try and make light of it.

"Sorry, guys. Didn't mean to scare you. I don't know what got into me. Hey, maybe I'm the one who should be applying to mountain rescue."

"Scrawny guy like you? Maybe if they need some pussycats rescuing from up a tree," Logan replied.

Collins allowed himself a small smile and concentrated on getting through the last few feet of tunnel. He was coated in sweat. He could feel it running down his forehead. He chided himself for not wearing a bandana under his hard hat to keep the sweat out of his eyes. He could feel it on his body too, under his shirt, he felt damp and sore. Sore? Sweat didn't normally make him feel sore. He identified a site of increasing pain in his side.

"Ow ... ahhh ... Jesus." Collins squirmed forward. Something—it felt like acid—was burning his abdomen, and the searing sensation was growing. He fought forward with all his might to get away from it. But he could not. It was moving with him. It felt like someone was holding a flaming torch to his side. The pain raked his skin. It was unbearable. He could hear himself screaming, feel himself fighting forward. He shattered his headlamp against a jutting rock and plastic shards rained down on his face as, instantly, utter darkness fell. He was sightless in the dark with blistering, fiery agony eating through his side.

Somehow, he found himself in open space. He had reached the chamber at the end of the tunnel. He ripped off his shirt and flung it away from him. The pain in his side did not abate. Touching his skin, he felt a slimy substance burn his fingertips. How to wipe it off? He crouched down and felt on the floor for his discarded shirt. Finally, weeping with relief, his fingers brushed cloth. He grabbed the shirt and felt for the areas on it that were not covered in slime. Wiping his side, he did not know if he was wiping away the slime or his own blood, or maybe both, but the pain eased. He wiped as much as his tender skin could stand and carefully wiped slime from his fingers too, then threw his shirt away from him.

Finally, the shouting from Logan and Surtees broke through his confusion, coming to him out of the darkness.

"I'm okay. It's okay," he called. "There's something in the tunnel, something, I don't know. It burned me pretty good."

"What? What do you mean? Burned you? What was it?" Logan's voice was a calming sound in the pitch black.

"Some kind of slimy gunk. In the tunnel wall, it must've been. Came out as I went past it. After my ...

episode."

"Collins, where was it? Was it in the rock I wanted to to sample?" Surtees this time.

"Yeah, I reckon."

"How are you doing?" Logan again. "Can you come back?"

"I'm not going past that slime again." Collins faintly heard Logan cursing.

"I smashed my lamp. Can you guys shine a light down the tunnel for me?" A moment later, Collins could see a patch of wall that was slightly less black than its surroundings.

He gingerly felt his side. It was wet, with blood he assumed, as it did not burn his fingers. The slime must have eaten through his skin. The ache from it was only tolerable because it was less painful than the feeling of being burned alive he had had before.

"Collins, you can't come back, I can't fit through to get you, and that slime could burn Surtees. I'm going for help," Logan's voiced echoed.

"Okay, I guess Marsh might have some ideas."

"I'll be back as fast as I can."

"Collins?" Surtees called.

"Uhuh?"

"You're at risk of shock, you know? I know you haven't got anything to cover yourself with, but ... just keep talking to me, okay?"

"I know. Okay." But he couldn't think of anything to say.

"You got a wife, Collins?"

"No ... no girlfriend either. Got a kid I see pretty regular. You?"

"Yeah, I'm married. My husband's dean of my university."

"Cool."

"Well, I get my research funded."

A wave of pain overcame Collins and he gasped. He grasped his head in his arms, willing himself not to touch his side.

"Kids?" he called through gritted teeth.

"Not yet."

Collins could not think of what else to say to

maintain the conversation that could be keeping him alive. Neither could Surtees, apparently, for a while, then,

"That stuff that slimed you, I'm sorry. I had no idea it would do that."

Through the ache that radiated from his wound Collins managed to reply, "You know what it is?"

"No, I haven't much idea at all. If it's the same stuff in the rock samples I examined topside, I just know it's got some organic compounds no one's ever seen before. It's amazing stuff."

"Amazingly fucking painful."

"Yeah, I'm sorry. Like I said, I didn't know it could do that. What I've seen so far is clearly only the residue of the organism or organisms that you encountered."

"Uhuh." Another wave of pain. "Oh, Christ." Collins wondered how long it would take for help to come. And then what? He could not get out, and no one would be able to get through to him without sliding through the acid slime. Healthy, he could stay here indefinitely while they passed food and water to him, but with the wound on his side, he was not so confident about his chances.

"Collins? You still with me?" He started awake. He had been drifting off. He must try to stay awake.

"Yeah, yeah, I'm still here. I'm going nowhere."

"If it's any consolation, that stuff that burned you, some of the compounds are linked with enhanced cell efficiency. If it's in your blood, it might actually be helping you."

"I'd rather be un-slimed and inefficient, to be honest."

"Yeah, well, I can see why you say that."

The conversation lapsed into silence again.

"Did you breathe it in before you had that panic attack? ... Collins? ... Collins?"

***

It was a sound that brought him back to consciousness, followed by pain. But he quickly stifled his groan as the memory of where he was, and what the sound must mean, returned. The noise was not coming from the tunnel he had come through, at the end of which Surtees presumably waited for Logan. It was coming from the other side of the chamber, from one of the three openings he had found before. And it was the sound of something sliding and scuffling toward him, through the darkness. Something big.

Collins strained to see. The only light was the palest shimmer from the narrow tunnel, where Logan or

Surtees had put a lamp. It was not really enough to see anything by, but Collins thought there was a blacker patch of black moving across the floor. What the hell it was he had no clue. Some critter of the deep earth, attracted maybe by all the shouting they had been doing, probably. As the hairs lifted on the back of his neck and beads of sweat formed on his forehead, the only thing Collins knew was that that thing, whatever it was, could probably see, or hear, or smell a hell of a lot better than he could. That it already knew exactly where he was and was coming over to ... what?

Running was out of the question. His only safe route contained acid slime. In the other unexplored tunnels he could get lost, or fall into an unseen chasm, or meet a hundred more of that creature's friends and relatives. He could call Surtees, but what could she do? And calling out might give the final clue to his whereabouts, just in case the deep cave beast was wondering. His only option was to strike first, to kill or disable the thing before it had a chance to hurt him.

Slowly it advanced, shuffling and dragging itself along. Collins had only his ears to guide him, but he knew he had to hit it hard, and make the blow count. Once hit, who knew what the animal might do to retaliate. The sound grew louder as the beast drew nearer. Collins could tell it was nearly upon him. He readied his fist. It sounded like it was inches from him. He struck out with all his might into the darkness. Yes!

His fist connected with skin and bone. The creature fell like a nine pin and lay still.

Collins' relief overwhelmed him. First the panic attack, then the slime, and now this? But he had killed the beast or at least knocked it out so it could not call its buddies to the feast.

A small thought niggled at him. Hitting that creature had felt familiar somehow. What the hell was that thing? Collins slid his fingers across the tunnel floor, tentatively probing for the edge of the animal. It was so still there probably was not any danger of rousing it. He touched its skin, which felt rough and very strange. Not scale, or skin or fur, but ... Realisation began to dawn. He felt further. It was not skin, it was cloth. Collin's felt up the 'beast's' chest, to its face. He felt ears, nose, mouth, eyes and several weeks' growth of beard.

"Oh, shit." Collins quickly felt the throat for a pulse.

"Thank God." He was still alive.

"Surtees," he called.

"COLLINS. You're alive. Thank goodness. You've been out for an hour or more—"

"I'm okay still, but, Surtees, I've found Tedeschi, or, rather—"

"WHAT? What did you say? You've found Ted? Ted's

there?"

"Yes, but—"

"TED? Can you hear me? Ted, I'm so sorry. I'm so sorry. Please forgive me. I love you. Ted?"

Collins was momentarily speechless.

"Ted? Are you there?"

"Surtees, he can't hear you. He's ... I ..."

"What's wrong? Ted, please, hang on, please—"

"He's okay ... ish. He's just ... fainted."

***

Collins leaned on Logan for support as the two of them made their way slowly back to base camp. The morphine shot Marsh had given him had made him woozy without seeming to take away much of the pain. Collins was glad to be out of the drama unfolding at the tunnel entrance, where they had left Marsh, the recovery team members, Surtees and the now-conscious Tedeschi. Marsh's face had indicated he found Surtees' sobbing over Tedeschi's prone body as embarrassing as Collins did.

"So Surtees and Tedeschi were—" Logan asked

"Having an affair, yes, as far as I could tell. He wanted her to leave her husband, but she wouldn't, because she'd lose her funding, be out of a job or whatever."

"Could her husband do that?"

"Don't know. I suppose so. He's a university dean, so—"

"So Tedeschi went off."

"Went off. I don't know why. Kill himself, space to think? Who knows. Got slimed, got lost, nearly died, I found him—"

"You knocked him out. After *he* found *you*."

"Well, technically ..."

"So what was it with the rocks?"

"The slime improves cell efficiency. Surtees didn't find out until she was back topside and looking at the samples she'd taken. She'd given Tedeschi up for dead, but when she saw the results from analysing those samples, she thought there might be just the slimmest chance he was still alive."

"Huh. That's why she snuck off this morning."

"Yeah, she must've gone back to where she'd got her

samples from the first time, wondering if Tedeschi had passed that way. Hoping to see something. I don't know. She was crazy with guilt and grief, I think. Maybe she should have just told someone her theory."

"Well, I don't believe it even though it's true."

"Yeah." Collins nodded.

They walked slowly on. It was going to be a long haul to get to the surface with his injured side, Collins thought, even with Marsh's expert medical care. He hoped Tedeschi would make it. The poor guy looked like a skeleton. There had been no problem getting him through the tunnel, once Marsh had contained the slime with plastic spray for stabilising loose rock.

"Hey, Collins," Logan broke into his thoughts.

"What?"

"You made the cave biologist cry *again*."

Red Ochre

Dangling in mid-air, terrified, it all came flooding back to me. I was out on the Martian plain again, my respirator broken; nothing but red rocks and dust between me and the horizon, under a pink sky. I could hear my dry, strained breathing, feel my chest heaving involuntarily as my lungs shuddered and bucked, straining for air; my body bypassing my brain in an uncontrollable fight for life.

Then I was back in the cave, suspended by the rope linking me to Pietr. His screaming shout sounded faint as I reached for my knife. "No, no no," echoed round the cavern. But I had no choice. I'm no lightweight, and he was slipping perilously close to the edge of the hole I had tumbled through, dragged by my weight. Better one of us falling than two. It took five seconds, maybe longer, to slice through the rope. The last threads snapped, and down I fell.

When I came to Pietr's form was the first thing I saw. Framed by the edge of the hole that had opened beneath me on our climb, his head and shoulders were silhouetted against the shaft of sunlight pouring into the cave.

I cursed inwardly, remembering the patch of earth and scree in a dip on the mountainside. An easy spot, I had thought, to rest up a moment. I had expected it to be a little loose. I had not expected it to collapse beneath me. I should not have taken the risk. This was supposed to be a relaxing recreational hike and climb. Nothing too challenging. Part of my therapy. But I had shown poor judgment, again. I wondered if I would always been so unfit to perform my duty.

I groaned, and shifted my head.

"Inge," called Pietr, "can you hear me? Are you okay? Have you broken anything?"

I coughed, and pain leaped in my chest. I winced and breathed gently. "How long have I been out?"

"Just a couple of minutes. Are you bleeding?"

"Don't think so." I sat up, moving slowly. I held out my hands and wriggled my fingers. I rotated my ankles. Nothing seemed badly damaged. My back throbbed. I pulled off my climbing helmet, and thanked my lucky stars I had been wearing it. The back of it was crushed in. I blinked and looked around, but could see little but darkness.

Reality began to settle in. We were in the middle of nowhere, on a mountainside, and it was late afternoon.

"What are we going to do?" I called.

"There's no other way out?"

I stood up carefully, and blinked hard. The cavern gradually became visible. I looked down, and a thrill of fear passed through me. I was not on the floor of the cave, but on a ledge. If I had fallen just half a metre out from where I was standing, I would have dropped another 10 metres, probably to my death.

"I don't think so. No light I can see other than through that damned hole," I called.

"You'd better not risk trying to find another escape route. You could get lost, and maybe no one would find you. I'll drop a rope and pull you up."

"You'll never do it. I weigh almost as much as you. And what if you fall in trying? Both of us would be stuck in here. With no phone signal." That had been my idea. To escape from all signs of civilisation and get back to the natural Earth I had missed so much in my nineteen months on Mars. To explore one of the few remaining truly wild areas, the South African wilderness. What the hell had I been thinking?

"Maybe you're right," said Pietr. "Is there a wall near the edge of the hole you can support yourself against as I pull?"

The cavern spread out around me, its grey walls distant from the hole in the roof. Climbing out would require an impossible feat.

"It's not going to happen," I called.

We were silent, though we both knew the only answer. Pietr would have to descend the mountain alone and hike to the closest area with phone coverage, about 10 hours away. I was going to be in the cavern overnight at the very least.

"Watch out," called Pietr. "I'm going to throw some things down for you."

"Okay, but throw them on this side. There's a drop just in front of me."

Energy bars hit the ground next to me, followed by Pietr's jacket.

"Don't leave me this, " I said. "You'll need it on your hike."

"I've got a spare sweater back at the tent. Catch this." A dark, cylindrical object fell. Pietr's flashlight.

"With your flashlight as well, you should have light all night," he said. "Now, move out the way."

A dull thunk signaled his water bottle smacking onto the dusty ledge.

"Pietr! You'll need this, too."

"I'll manage. That's it. That should be all you need. You'll be fine. As soon as I can get a signal, I'll ca l the emergency services. I can tell them exactly where you are. They'll fly a helicopter out to you as soon as it's light. You'll be out of here before tomorrow lunchtime, and we'll go straight to a bar and laugh about all this over a beer."

I looked up, trying to make out Pietr's face against the warm, golden sunlight; trying to fight back the vision of the dull, rust-red Martian landscape that reared up before my eyes, and the memory of a thin, bitter, icy atmosphere biting into my throat and lungs. I heard the tinny clunk of my space helmet hitting the rocky ground. I squeezed my eyes shut and willed my racing heart to slow.

"Pietr—" My voice choked to a stop.

"Inge, you'll be okay." His words were warm and full of concern.

I looked up at him again, ashamed of the tears

wetting my cheeks and hoping he could not see them.

"I'd better get going straightaway," he said.

"I know."

He stood up, and his movement scattered dust through the beams of sunlight that shone into the cavern.

"Pietr," I said. My voice sounded weak as it echoed from the walls.

"Yes, Inge?"

"Good luck."

I hugged myself as my old, good friend disappeared from sight.

***

I sought a way down from the ledge. There was only an hour or so of daylight left, and if I slept where I was I risked falling to my death during the night. I gathered the supplies Pietr had left me into his jacket, and shuffled down the slope a few metres. My eyes had grown accustomed to the dim light, and I could see a gradual descent to the floor on the other side of the cavern. Clutching the bundle of supplies to me, I edged slowly over.

There seemed to be no living thing in the cavern but me. Nothing moved or grew, and the cave floor looked bare. I wondered if maybe I was the first living creature ever to set foot on it. The air smelled stale and strange.

Reaching solid, level, safe ground was a minor relief. I looked up at the hole in the cavern roof, which was now smaller and dimmer. The light that shone through it was tinged pink with the encroaching sunset. I cast about for somewhere to spend the night.

Where I was seemed as good a place as any. I dropped Pietr's jacket containing my supplies and his water bottle to the floor, and sat down. I took a swig of water from my own bottle strapped to my side, but decided not to eat anything. I might have to make my food and water last longer than I hoped.

More depressing than going without food and water was the thought that I faced an unknown number of hours in this precarious situation. My flashbacks to the accident during my Mars mission were triggered by stress, but they had been occurring less frequently of late, and I had finally begun to hope I might get well enough to work again. Going into space was out of the question, but they might have given me a lab job or something; something to stop me feeling such a useless failure. Enduring a survival situation like this was going to set my recovery back months, maybe forever.

As if on cue, my mind threw me back to Mars. I was

on a transporter, trundling over a barren plain. As the mission geologist, it was my responsibility to collect a wide variety of rock samples and test them for minerals and biosignatures. I already had a couple of samples. Collecting the most recent one I had taken a small tumble, but had not thought much more of it.

I saw an outcrop that stood out a deeper red than its surroundings. I stopped the transporter and hopped off, grabbing my chisel and hammer from the seat pocket. I decided to make this the last sample before going back to base camp as I was at the limit of the safe range, according to transporter batteries' remaining power and my respirator's oxygen level.

Absorbed in chipping away at the rock and bathed in Mar's red-tinged light, I failed to notice the red alarm light when it flicked on inside my helmet. Nor could I hear any sounds outside my suit, such as the hiss of pressurized oxygen mix leaking from my respirator. It was only when the alarm light began to flash that it attracted my attention. The oxygen gauge dropped as I watched it in disbelief. The alarm warning had not sounded. Was my suit's speaker-mic broken as well as my respirator? Would the base hear my distress call? I had no choice but to try, and pray that they would get to me before I ran out of air.

The peak of the flashback hit. I was lying on the ground. I had torn off my space helmet in a panicked, irrational effort to breathe, and I was gasping, gasping, gasping, and no one had come. I was going to die alone on that desolate planet, a hundred million miles from warm, living Earth, thriving with people. A chip of deep red Martian rock in my outstretched hand was the last thing I remembered before passing out.

As the flashback faded, I realised something pointed was digging into my backside. I shuffled over a little, only to encounter another pointed edge. I shuffled farther, but the ground seemed to be full of sharp objects just below the dusty surface. I traced the edge of one and smoothed the dust from it. It was a piece of shaped stone. I worked it free from the ground and held it up to the light.

Breaking off the compacted dirt, I saw at once it was a point—a prehistoric arrowhead or spear tip. The shape was not quite symmetrical. A too-large chip had been struck from one side, making the edge uneven. I unearthed another point, and another. Each was not quite perfect. I was sitting on a prehistoric flintknapper's rubbish heap. It was a discovery I had dreamed of as a child, before my eyes had turned from what lay beneath the Earth's surface to the secrets of the night sky.

It might have been tens of thousands of years ago, but the cave had once been occupied. I looked around me with new eyes. The sun had ceased to shine directly in through the hole, and was providing only a fading glow. I took off my climbing gloves and turned on my flashlight. Its beam revealed a rocky but otherwise featureless, slightly sloping floor and irregularly contoured walls filled with pits. The far reaches of the cavern were in darkness. I got up to explore.

Keeping to the cavern's edge, I walked slowly forward, swinging the flashlight beam over the walls and floor. It all seemed unremarkable until—I gasped. Hands. The outlines of hands, traced by a delicate, fine, even spray of red ochre. I had seen pictures, but they had not, could not, compare with the reality before me. Sharply defined by the deep red pigment, the hands looked as though they had been placed there yesterday. Hands broad and slim, large and small. Unmistakably, undeniably human. Many people had been in this cave, maybe living, eating, sleeping here. I held my hand over the outline of another, imagining, trying to connect with, that far distant relative. But I knew better than to contaminate the painting by touching it. Instead, I lightly rested my hand in a notch to the right of the image.

My fingertips brushed a loose piece of rock, and I drew it out and shone my flashlight on the fragment. My heart leaped and a small cry escaped me. It was a piece of red ochre. A pattern of lines had been scratched down one side, and the end had been worn away. It was the base of the paint that had been sprayed over the outstretched hands. After finishing the art work, the artist had placed the pigment in a handy nook, and I, tens of thousands of years later, had drawn it out again.

For a moment, I do could nothing but stand there, holding the piece of ochre. My tears splashed onto the red stone, and I wiped my sleeve across my face. I turned the fragment over in my hand and examined the delicate pattern. Protocols dictated I should immediately replace the ochre exactly where I had found it, but I gazed at it for an age. Finally, I put it back in the niche where it had lain for so long.

I made a mental note of the exact placement of the pigment, and looked up. The sky through the hole was dark, and stars glimmered. I decided to save my flashlight batteries and explore farther tomorrow. I returned to the place I'd left Pietr's jacket, and ate an energy bar and drank some water before finding a smooth area of ground to try to get some sleep.

***

It was a dream. It *had* to be a dream, and yet ...

I seemed to wake to the soft touch of hands on my body, feeling, probing, examining. I jerked in surprise and opened my eyes. Naked, dark people squatted around me, their deep brown eyes searching mine and roaming over me. We looked at each other for a moment before the hands reached out to feel me again.

"Hey," I said, and pushed them away. The skin was rough, and their fingernails were black and broken. I sat up. The cave was lit, not brightly, but enough to see by. Daylight came from above and to the right, through a low opening. I could also hear water trickling. The people around me spoke to each other, and the language was like nothing I had ever heard. It was musical, and sometimes the speech sounded more like singing than speaking. A woman reached out to touch my hair.

"Hey, please don't—" But they did not stop. I sighed. "Oh, okay."

I sat, submissive, as the people fulfilled their curiosity about me. I took the opportunity to look closely at them in turn. Their hair was black and tightly curled, and their skin was ebony. Sinewy muscles moved beneath the adults' skin, and the children were long-limbed and graceful. So these were the prehistoric people my mind had conjured up in response to my situation? I smiled to myself and decided to go with the flow, wondering what other details my subconscious would manifest.

I got up, and the people rose from their haunches too. As I walked to the place where I had found the cave painting, they followed me as a crowd. There were about twenty-five of them, from the three or four babes clutched to their mothers' breasts, to an old man with streaks of gray running through his hair. The painting was exactly as I had seen it before I fell asleep, except the colour was deeper and more vivid. The chattering and nodding increased as we all regarded the outlines of hands. A young woman stepped forward and placed her hand over an outline on the wall. She smiled and spoke to me in her sing-song language.

"I so wish I could understand you," I said.

It was the most beautiful dream of my life. I drank from the rill running along the floor at the edge of the cavern. I ate the tough meat and flavourful roots the people roasted over a fire. I played with the dusty babies and examined the people's artifacts: bows, arrows, spears, bags of chewed leather, necklaces of seashells strung on thongs. I walked out of the cavern and explored the surrounding countryside. The air was like wine, rich and clean, and the landscape alive with plant, animal and insect life. The people seemed puzzled, but tolerant of me.

As the daylight faded, I remembered something. I found the nook that had held the red ochre. It was still there, looking exactly as before. I ran my fingertips over its warm, smooth surface. In my dream, it was not a precious archaeological artifact. On a whim, I put it in my pocket.

When all the people lay sleeping around me, I tried

to stay awake and make the dream last as long as I could, but I eventually awoke cold and stiff in the wan light of morning, alone and lonely, waiting and hoping for rescue.

Much later, I heard the distant whirr of helicopter blades.

***

Pietr was wrong. It was not until the evening that we made it to a bar to drink and laugh over my poor judgment, or bad luck, or whatever it was. And I did laugh, louder and harder than I had laughed in a long time, till my stomach ached and I wept. Pietr related how he had been looking at me when I had suddenly got the most surprised look he had ever seen in his life, and then I had disappeared as though I had dropped through a stage trap door. And how I had tried to drag him down with me, 'because you've always wanted to get me alone in a dark place, haven't you, Inge?' as he wiggled his eyebrows suggestively.

It was not until I was thoroughly drunk that I realized I had not had a flashback since I had woken up that morning. My befuddled mind wandered back to the cavern. I recalled the miracle of finding the red ochre in the nook where an artist had placed it tens of millenia before, and my tinge of sorrow at replacing it there.

I recalled the people in my dream. They had been

few, and just starting out in a fresh new world. They had done things wrong and made mistakes and had accidents that maybe they could or could not have prevented. But they had survived and won through.

Pietr was even drunker than me, but somehow we managed to weave our way to the right hotel. On the way, the cold night air penetrated my numbed senses, and I pushed my hands into my pockets. Smooth and solid, the red ochre met my chilled knuckles.

Return of the Prodigals

They brought the freaks to Earth on shuttles from the Space Station. They were lying on long gurneys, encased in clear plastic domes. The medical staff that wheeled them into hospital looked like midgets in comparison. The beds were nine or ten feet long, yet only just long enough. The freaks were naked beneath their white sheets and you could see areas of skin—a deep, dull red, like the planet they had come from. Oxygen masks covered their faces, but I remember noticing their long, black hair.

At the time, I was angry. Who wouldn't be? It was only natural.

Three of them were DOA, the news report said.

My rota included the ward set aside for them. I got there early, about five a.m. They were sound asleep despite the beep-beep-beep of the monitoring equipment. Only six of the specially-made beds fitted in that ten-bed room, and then only awkwardly. I had to reprogram the cleaning bots to reactive sensitivity, which makes them take longer. Another bloody expense and inconvenience, that's what I thought.

A female was nearest the door where I loitered as I waited for the bots to finish. She was spark out, like the rest. Her long, long, red arms lay on top of the sheet, and her head was turned away, thick black hair streaming over her pillow. The line from her mask snaked over her hair to the tank beside her bed, and another for urine fed a bag attached to the side. Heart, oxygen, breathing machines, the works. I kept looking and looking, trying to take in how long and thin she was.

As her head turned and her eyes opened I froze. There was almost no white in them, just deep brown that was almost black, so you couldn't see the pupils. Like cats eyes in the dark. I couldn't help but stare. She tried to say something, but the mask was over her mouth, and each bed was still covered in a dome. I looked away. I cleaned their ward earlier after that, so I could be sure they would all be asleep.

I got my notice. I'd seen it coming. Who needed sanitation staff any more? Sanobots had been in the pipeline for ages. Robots too small to see, unlike the decrepit old machines I had to use. It was only a matter of time before I was made redundant. Set sanobots loose, and they silently clean 24/7 without anyone even noticing them.

Two weeks notice, they said. No, there were no other duties for me, they said. Two weeks was all I was entitled to, and they acted like they were doing me a big favour letting me work them out.

I didn't tell my kids. What would have been the point? I think maybe Tila, my oldest, guessed something was up. She gave me an extra tight hug as she said goodnight that night. I hugged her back and breathed in the scent of her hair, trying to commit it to memory.

I set out to pay the freaks a visit next day. I don't know what exactly I was planning to do. Rip out some lines, push some beds over. The unfairness of it filled me with fury. I couldn't understand why they got so much money spent on them, keeping them alive. And even if they survived the first weeks, they were going to live like cripples the rest of their lives. Why should my taxes pay for them? Charity begins at home. There was I, two kids to feed and their father long gone, and now no job to keep the wolf from the door. I didn't know what was going to become of us. I might even have to give the kids up. We didn't owe the freaks anything. Their ancestors took their chances when they agreed to go out to Mars. If the colony failed, that was their look out.

And as for those smarmy gits with degrees telling me

to retrain—as what? I'd never been academic, and these days being good with your hands didn't count for much. There was always a machine or a computer programme that could do it better than you. All I could expect was a life on Subsistence Income, which, with the cost of things these days, was no life at all.

I heard them talking as I got near the ward. A high-pitched, twittering sound. People had said they spoke English, but I couldn't make out a word. The domes and masks had been off for a week, and the bed heads were raised, so they could look around. Silence fell as I walked in.

Like I said, I don't know what I was planning to do. I was seething with rage. I stood in the doorway, screwing myself up to punish these scroungers. They were that weak, I could have killed one of them easily. They were too weak even to feed themselves. They watched me, sideways on. Probably wondering who the hell I was.

They all looked the same. The only female was the one I'd seen first, nearest the door, but they all had the same long hair, and wrinkled skin, like they were really old, though the news reports said they were all in their twenties. The final generation of a failed colony. The Martians had stopped having kids when we told them that we couldn't afford to continue sending supply ships; that the experiment was over.

What I wanted to say was: You're not wanted here, why have you come? We're spending millions keeping you alive. Why didn't you stay where you belong? But the words wouldn't come out.

I saw the protest banners through the window. Martians Go Home, they said. The faces of the protesters were screwed up and ugly. Whatever they were shouting couldn't be heard through the soundproofing, but the hate was clear enough. Fists waving in the air, mouths open, screaming and shouting. Mean, angry people. Why the police let them stand right outside the window I didn't know. Martians go home? That was a bit stupid, I thought. How were they supposed to do that? There weren't going to be any more ships to Mars.

In my last week at the hospital I didn't have much to do. The sanobots were working well, and you could already see the effects. All those little out of the way places where my bots couldn't reach were suddenly clean. Everything seemed brighter, newer.

I was on general dogsbody duties. They told me to set up an interface in the Martians' room to screen a link to the ones who'd stayed behind. The time delay meant they couldn't really talk to each other, but they could watch the video and type messages.

I stuck around after I'd set it up. I didn't have anything else to do, and I had to take it back in two hours. They were all pretty excited. Well, not so much excited as agitated. Chattering in that weird accent they had, and tapping away on keyboards.

Looking at the background to the Martians on the screen, I studied Mars closely for the first time. I'd never really been interested in the Martian colony. It had always been just something on the news every so often. I'd never seen the fuss. The place seemed to be nothing but low domes, and desert to the horizon. No wonder some of the younger ones wanted to take their chances on Earth. But then again, looking at the state of them, I could also see why most had chosen to stay behind.

The female Martian in the ward didn't show much reaction until a face appeared on the screen, close up and talking. Another female. We couldn't hear her of course. Just see her moving lips and the tears pouring down her face. The female at our end got all frantic and started jabbering something I couldn't make out. She was talking to me, like she wanted something.

"What?" I walked over. "What is it?"

One of the others spoke. He'd learned Earth English. Proper English.

"She wants you to push her bed over to the screen."

"Why? Can't she see it properly?"

He didn't answer.

It was probably against hospital policy, but I was out of a job in a week anyway, and I was curious to see what she would do. Their monitoring equipment had been removed, so I didn't have to disconnect her from anything, which would have brought the nurses running. I maneuvered her bed over, taking care not to crash into the screen.

When I got her there I stood back. The same expressive face remained on the screen, talking silently. Our female spoke to me again.

"She wants you to push her closer," said the other Martian.

I pushed her right up against the screen, so that her bed was lengthwise against it. It drew complaints from the others who couldn't see properly, but she ignored them. She lifted her hand, trembling with the effort. She placed her fingertips on the talking woman's face and a high, moaning sound escaped her lips.

"Who's that on the screen? Do you know?" I asked the English-speaking one.

"Her mother," he said.

***

Mr. Busybody from HR stopped me on my way home

that night, offering me a job caring one-to-one for a Martian. Soon they would be strong enough to go into assisted housing. The job was the usual thing - toileting, feeding, washing.

"Think about it overnight and let me know tomorrow," he said. "Jobs get snapped up these days, as you know."

"Okay, I'll think about it."

He paused, apparently waiting for something.

"Thanks," I said.

Satisfied, he walked away.

"Hey," I called, as he was about to turn the corner. "I thought about it. I'll do it. For the female one."

Her name is Frirash.

Never in Fear Fly to the Woods

He ties binding around the ends of his sleeves and trouser legs, pulls on gloves and a hat, winds material around his face, leaving his eyes and nostrils free. Outside, the hives hum. The heat of two suns burns through his hat. He dampens a rag, takes a spark striker from his pocket, sets the rag to smolder. This much, he knows. The proper equipment was lost in the crash, but he can improvise.

Stupefied with smoke, the bees drone lazily as he lifts a lid on a hive. Honeycombs are growing. All seems well, but he isn't sure what he is looking for. Bees sit at the entrances to the hives, cooling the interiors with their beating wings.

Back at the wrecked ship, he grinds the rag beneath

his boot, smothering its glow in the dirt. The white, dusty ground throws up a blinding glare. Squatting on his heels, he pulls his hat low over his eyes. In the distance, a work party is returning from the fields. Shoulders hunched, feet dragging, they approach.

Ship's captain Hannah, ex-captain, unelected leader, breaks away, heads over, drops down beside him. Legs sprawling akimbo, she rests her hands on the ground behind her, flinches at the heat, and folds her arms loosely. A patina of dust clings to her face, eyebrows, eyelashes. The odor of sweat she exudes is mixed with the scent of the fields; the strange, alien scent he cannot get used to. The scent that raises the hair on the back of his neck.

"How are they doing?" she asks, nodding towards the hives.

"Well, I think. As far as I can tell, I mean."

She draws a boot heel along the ground, making a furrow in the dirt.

"How about the bean crop?" he asks.

Her mouth twists. "Surviving. I think they'll flower. Will the bees be ready?"

He shrugs, reluctant to commit.

"Have you talked to her recently?" she asks.

He shakes his head, squints at the sun nearest the horizon. The air blazes blue-green tints. The lower edge of the sun shimmers. Its brilliant brother is looking over its shoulder. In the heat, he shivers.

"I don't know how you can all ..." he says.

"What?"

He studies his hands. "What's it like, out there?"

She grimaces. "Hot. Dry. Lifeless. We'll green this place, though, Robert."

She stands, and doesn't bother to brush the dirt from her clothes. "Talk to her. We can't afford to keep her going much longer. We need the power for other things."

He does not respond. He does not move. He screws up his eyes as he looks once more at the horizon.

***

Inside the ship, he pauses, waiting for his eyes to adjust to the dimness. He stands at the centre of a tall, cylindrical room. Vertical, body-sized compartments line the walls around him. Above his head, they rise in tiers, linked by narrow walkways. Most are open, vacant, dark; their contents disgorged. He climbs. The metal rungs of the ladder are cool and smooth against his hot, dusty hands. He stops at a closed compartment. He thumbs a series of buttons, and a panel opens at head height. A woman's face is behind the glass. Her eyes are closed, her lips relaxed, almost smiling. Her ebony hair lies on her shoulders like wreaths of silk. He speaks into a mic:

"Maggie?"

Her lips do not move, but a reply comes through a speaker. "Yes, Robert?" The voice is electronic, but mimics the woman's tone and cadence.

"What are you doing?" he asks.

"I'm charming the bees."

"Charming ...?"

A laugh. "I'm a fool, I know. They've swarmed, you see? You throw some earth under your right foot and say:

I've got it, I've found it:

Lo, earth masters all creatures

It masters evil, it masters deceit

It master's humanity's greedy tongue.

"Then you take some more earth and scatter it over the bees and say:

Sit, wise women settle on earth:

Never in fear fly to the woods.

Please be mindful of my welfare

As all men are of food and land.

It's Anglo-Saxon. It's just a fancy. See, they're starting to settle on a branch."

His posture relaxes. He smiles, closes his eyes and rests a hand on the wall. "I see. What's it about?"

"The charm? Hmm ... The earth's control over us and the bees? That's my interpretation, anyway. The earth helps to settle them in one place, so I can take them to a new hive. Those Anglo-Saxons were so clever. How did they know the workers were female, I wonder?"

"You scatter earth over them?"

"Just lightly. I'm sure they would settle anyway." She laughs again.

"Maggie?"

"Yes?"

"Where are you? What can you see?"

"I can see the wood, of course. What an odd thing to

ask. Can't you see for yourself? Robert? Where are you, Robert? Where are you?"

He closes the panel.

***

On a bed fashioned from a pile of blankets and clothes, in a side room, he sits and writes in a notebook. His fingers are clumsy and his handwriting poorly formed. He pauses and frowns, sighs and closes the book. He pours sugar solution into a container and goes outside. The nearer sun has set and the farther is drawing close to the horizon. Cool breezes flow towards it, drying the sweat on the back of his neck. Already the bees are thick around the remains of this morning's solution, dipping their proboscies into the sticky patches.

He pours the solution into the feeders and steps back, watching the steady lines of bees flying to and from the hives. More than a mile distant, a patch of dark green marks the crop fields. His eyes travel the distance from hives to fields and back again, avoiding the collection of mounds and headstones that lie at the midpoint. He takes off his hat and runs his fingers through his greasy hair.

Inside once more, he follows a ruined corridor. The floor is buckled, and in places the walls are pierced by joists. He opens a door, releasing the murmur of voices within. Men and women sit haphazardly around the room, in chairs, on the floor, or perched on dead instrument panels and lifeless consoles. They are eating from metal bowls.

"Robert, you'd better be quick, there's not much left," says a young woman in a dirty gray flight uniform.

He takes a bowl and spoon. Someone scoops out a ladle of stew for him. It is a mixture of grains and reconstituted dried vegetables. The texture is coarse, the taste bland. He grimaces as he forces it down.

"Joining us out in the fields tomorrow, Robert?" calls a sharp-faced man with a thin beard.

He shrugs and fills his mouth with another spoonful.

"Been missing you out there, Robert," says the man. "Need all the help we can get if we're gonna get this harvest in. Even a systems tech can dig, you know."

He chews. The room is quiet and the people watch him.

"There's some stew left if anyone's up for a second helping," says Hannah. Several people stand, and the conversations resume.

"Sure wish I could pull honeybee duty, relaxing in the cool shade all day," says the sharp-faced man, his drawling voice raised above the hubbub. The room becomes silent once more.

"Winston, you're on digging duty again tomorrow," snaps Hannah. The man curses and throws down his bowl, the remains of his stew splattering the floor. "And you'll clean that up now if you don't want to be digging all week." She turns to the crew.

"In case anyone else is as dumb as Winston, let me explain," she enunciates. "If this colony is going to be successful we have to grow our own food. If we're going to grow our own food we need bees to pollinate the crops. You think you'd rather be a beekeeper than a farmer? Do any of you have the first freaking idea how?" Lips set, her eyes roam the room. "Does anyone here want to go and talk to Maggie to find out? Raise your hand if you do. Anyone? Winston?" Winston keeps his head down and wipes the floor.

Hannah sits on the edge of a desk. "You're all tired, I know. You're tired and hot and sweaty, and you're sick of eating the same thing night after night. Things didn't go to plan. We crashed. We lost people and equipment we needed. Some of us lost people we loved. But what's happened has happened. There's no going back and there's no rescue mission that's going to get here before we're all dust. Wishing things were different won't change anything; it will just make you miserable." She stands. "So if anyone else is thinking how much better off they'd be if they were beekeeping, or weeding instead of digging, or cooking instead of cleaning, forget it. Every chore has to be done and the work is shared out fairly according everyone's experience and skills. For this colony to succeed we all have to do the work we can do."

After he's finished eating, he goes to Hannah. "I can do more," he says.

Her eyes search his. "Are you sure?"

"I think so." He looks down. "I can try."

She touches his upper arm. "We're sowing brassicas tomorrow. I'll send someone to collect you when the work team goes out."

***

When he opens the panel Maggie's face is exactly as before.

"What are you doing?" he asks.

"Packing. Five kilos!" Comes the voice from the speaker. "How to fit everything you want to take to a new world into five kilos of luggage? Five kilos for a lifetime of memories." A sigh. "Have you packed? What are you taking?" A pause. "Robert, where are you?"

His eyes close. "I'm here, Maggie. You just can't see me."

"What? Where are you? Don't do that. Come out. You're frightening me."

"I'm here. Don't be scared."

"Why can't I see you? Where are you?"

"I'm ... " His voice catches. "Maggie ..."

"Robert, what's wrong? Please tell me. Where are you hiding?"

He tries to speak, but cannot.

"You aren't here, are you? You're in my mind," she says. "Robert, are you a—a ghost? Have you died?"

He runs his sleeve across his eyes. He pinches his nose and wipes snot on his trouser leg. "I haven't died. I'm on Kepler 568c. We named it Perseverance." He screws his eyes shut and rubs them with his thumb and forefinger. "I reach into your memory. I'm sorry, I have to. You're the only one who knows how to care for the bees. Most of the stored data was destroyed."

Another silence. "That's ... not credible. No." A nervous laugh. "I'm imagining things. But I can hear you as clear as day. If this is a joke, please, come out now."

"I can't. I'm not there."

"You - you're from the future?"

"In a way. You're at the time before we left, right?"

"It's two days before launch."

A long silence. He leans against the metal and rests his forehead on his arm.

"Have I died?" The voice is quiet.

"We crashed. You didn't survive."

"I see." A pause. "I'd heard about this, but being on the other side ... Have you spoken to me before?"

"Many times."

"I don't remember?"

"You can't form new memories."

"Of course ... I never thought ... Have I already asked you if I'm dead?"

He doesn't answer.

"It must be hard for you," she says.

"It's ..." He swallows. "I miss you."

Silence.

"What's it like? Kepler—Perseverance? Is it how we imagined it?" she asks.

"It's hot, dry, barren. Where we are, anyway. With the land craft destroyed this area is where we have to try to build the colony. Perseverance is incredible. And terrifying."

"I wish I was there to see it with you."

He lifts his hand and rests it on the glass.

"What do you need to know about keeping bees?"

They talk. She says nothing he has not already written down. The conversation dries.

She says, "Robert, will you promise me something? When it's the last time, don't say goodbye."

***

"I hear you're joining our team today." The voice wakes him. He opens his eyes to see the young woman in the dirty gray flight uniform who spoke to him at dinner. She is standing above him. She smiles. "Morning."

He sits up.

"Morning, Lucy," he says.

"I'll wait for you outside. I've got your breakfast. Fill your water bottle. You're gonna need it."

A sliver of brilliant sunlight is peeking over the horizon. The air temperature is already rising. A group five of crew members wait for him as he tops up the bees' sugar solution.

"All set?" says Lucy.

He nods, though his heart is starting to race and his hands are clammy. He scans the view. It is a flat, pale shadow under the rising sun. Light washes over it, sparking flecks of silica in the bleached earth. Around the crop fields, the landscape is utterly barren.

He walks with the crew, but as he draws away from the crashed spacecraft his feet begin to slow and drag. The sharp scent of the alien earth nauseates him. His breathing quickens and his vision swims. He looks back. The downed ship seems to call him. The effort of turning back to face the way he is walking wrenches a gasp from him.

"Hey, Robert," says Lucy.

"What?" He has forgotten she is walking beside him.

"Tell me about the bees."

"The bees?"

"Yeah, I mean, there's a lot to it, right? I thought you just got them, and they did their thing, you know what I mean? But it seems like there's more to it than that. Am

I right?"

"The bees?" He focuses on her face, her eyes. "The bees are amazing."

"Really?"

"Yes, I didn't really understand before how organized they are. They have everything under control. Each type of bee has its role, and they all work so hard for the sake of the hive. They're hard-working, selfless ... impressive creatures all round."

"Well I'm sure looking forward to some honey."

"Ah yes, well, you'll have to wait a little while for that, I'm afraid. But I agree, we could do with some variation in our diet. But bees are about so much more than honey, you know, Lucy. They were almost an afterthought in the planning, as I understand it, but they're vital, absolutely vital." He squints at the dusty landscape. "We may even see one or two scouts out and about."

"Hey, I already have."

"You have?"

"Sure. We see them all the time, right guys?"

He has something to focus on. A distraction from the clammy terror rising in his throat. Looking for bees is how he makes to the area to be sown. Looking for bees is how he stands out on that flat ground, far distant from the ship, as the twin suns rise and pour down heat.

He draws a hoe through the soft, pale dirt, which parts like butter. He notices something. Within the fine, upturned soil are lumps the same colour as the dirt. They are uniform. He continues to hoe his line, the pale lumps falling to either side of the furrow he creates. At the end of the line he squats down and picks one up. He twirls it between his fingertips. It is smooth, and as long and thick as the last joint on his little finger.

Lucy's shadow falls over him.

"What've you got there?"

He stands and hands the object to her. She emits a low whistle.

"What is it?" he asks. "A cocoon of some sort? I thought there was nothing out here."

"So did everyone else." She turns. "Hey, guys, come look at this."

"You haven't seen these before? But there are so many of them."

"Nope. Looks like you're the lucky winner. You might just have found our first ever alien life form."

The rest of the work team arrive and begin to pick up lumps and examine them.

"Shit, I was forgetting," says Lucy. "Drop the cocoons, everyone. We've gotta stop touching them. We have no idea what's in them. The surface could be toxic or something. We have to go back and tell Hannah. Let's pack up and go, okay?

As they begin to shoulder their tools and walk away, he hangs back. He bends down and picks up one of the lumps. He cradles it in his hand. With his teeth he pulls the stopper from his water bottle, and douses the object with water.

Washed free of dirt, it glistens. The crew members are drawing away from him, but he stands, fascinated. Lucy turns and calls, telling him to catch up. He cannot take his eyes from the object in his hand. It twitches, and he nearly drops it. It jerks, splits open. He gasps.

Shimmering emerald and sapphire tissue expands and fills his palm. Slowly the tissue separates and takes form. Four wings, two on either side, translucent and fine as spider thread. Where the wings meet, a tiny, slim, softly furred black body squirms. Robert is mesmerised. The departing crew and the distant, crashed spaceship are forgotten. The heat, the alien scent, the two impossible suns are distant glimmers at the back of his mind. He sees nothing but the new life trembling in his hand.

The wings lift, flap, the bone-dry air drying them instantly. Tears fill his eyes.

He lifts the creature, holding his open palm to the sky. Two beats of its wings, and it is gone.

Thanks for reading!

Your honest review is welcome and much appreciated.

If you enjoyed *There Comes a Time* and would like to hear about other J.J. Green books, new releases, advanced reader opportunities and other interesting stuff, sign up to the mailing list here:

https://infinitebook.wordpress.com/

You'll receive a free ebook fantasy collection, *Dawn Falcon*.

(We won't send spam or pass on your details to a third party.)

Printed in Great Britain
by Amazon